# THE SEA IN THE RADIO

THE GERMAN LIST

JÜRGEN BECKER

*The Sea in the Radio*

JOURNAL SENTENCES

TRANSLATED BY ALEXANDER BOOTH

LONDON NEW YORK CALCUTTA

This publication has been supported
by a grant from the Goethe-Institut India

Grateful acknowledgement and thanks to the editors of *Chicago Review*
for publishing an excerpt of this translation in slightly different form.

**Seagull Books, 2021**

First published in German as *Im Radio das Meer* by Jürgen Becker
© Suhrkamp Verlag, Berlin, 2009

First published in English by Seagull Books, 2021
English translation © Alexander Booth, 2021

ISBN   978 0 8574 2 885 1

**British Library Cataloguing-in-Publication Data**
A catalogue record for this book is available from the British Library.

Typeset by Seagull Books, Calcutta, India
Printed and bound in the USA by Integrated Books International

# CONTENTS

Journal One

Expanses of snow push into the woods, but they don't get very far. The pinewoods, the ones that begin behind the Elbe, the river meadows.

Nothing marks a border's disappearance. As if there had never even been a border at all.

A pair of strokes, a drawing, you already see the beginnings of a fence, but it's not a fence.

One never saw them, the trains off behind the woods.

All the voices in one's head, and some that don't want to say a word.

Wild boar crossing the motorway. Mornings from right to left, evenings from left to right.

People come in, personnel emerge. Who'll be needed is still unclear.

It was always nighttime when Father came home from his travels.

From the West you came into the East. From the East you went into the West.

In-between the suburbs, where the countryside disappears.

It's not dark enough. Before then, the owl will say nothing.

Spring-guns protected the yard. Was it a yard? Yes, it was a yard.

The off-road vehicle comes closer. Idles for a while at the edge of the woods. Crawls along, then comes back to a halt.

Whenever a story began, he never quite understood where it was supposed to go.

A few photographs which have been removed from the album.

Is there a list of the apartments that have been cleared?

A dead man's birthday. The moss in a vase. A lane straight through the woods.

*Sunday. The world is seven days old.*

Once again, someone has discovered something which had been neglected.

The increasing glow of the hedgerows, aglow in the light of the dimming sun.

Here's a photograph of what was once your house. Thank you. But, in the photo, that wasn't our house.

The letterbox had frozen shut; the one next to it could still be opened.

People would get together and begin to talk about the weather.

Whoever intends to participate must participate.

Snowshine. Drop of sun.

Open the window. When the cold air comes in, close it again.

Every year the painter sits in his yard. Sometimes he walks around. Wherever he stops, he sits down. And begins a new painting of the yard.

In the middle of a lake, you don't see anything that marks a border, and the ducks swim back and forth.

Evening reels the shadows in.

The soliloquy of the motorway.

People sitting together. One of them gets up and goes outside. He's got a job to do and doesn't come back.

If everyone conforms to all the signals and rules, nothing can go wrong.

They are the smallest birds, the ones in the thorn bushes.

Let her go.

Ever more people stream into the hall. It's not quite full when the roof collapses.

At the kiosk, a light's still on.

Another funeral. You see each other every few months, split back up, then say, See you next time.

Someone says, For ten years now I've begun each day as if it were the last.

At the kiosk, a light is always on, even when it's closed.

What does voluntarily mean when they say that the apartments have voluntarily been cleared?

Two fatalities, two survivors. The survivors have to figure out what kind of relationship there was between the deceased.

Neighbours standing around discussing neighbours.

Someone told the truth and since then have only known aggravation.

One game after another lost, in the end the trainer said he wanted to teach his players the meaning of politeness, tolerance, brotherly love.

The newspaper's incessant sneer.

Now it's dark enough. Straining our ears to hear what is outside.

The music doesn't stop, and the passages are endless,
as they are circular.

The stairs lead up to a ramp, but after the ramp
there's nothing.

He's scribbling. Everything crooked and canted.

Glass is democratic, the architect says, stone fascistic.

Sea mail. The symbol for sea mail is yellow, like land mail.
Airmail's is blue. Blue like the airmail.

If you're looking for the off-road vehicle, it's in front of
a stream now.

A moment's wavering . . . but not so that later they'll say
one wavered too long.

Then go on and explain why there was nothing to explain.

That young girl is this old woman.

It's winter, and there's a Finnish translation on the table.

The old iron stove is smoking. It's got to be the wood.
It's just been cut, it's green wood. Green wood is too new.

The caged chickens have been set loose again. The loose
chickens have been caged again.

Maybe it starved to death, the dead hawk.

Father wouldn't say much when he got home. The first thing he'd do was darken the windows.

The oxen that pulled the carts knew the way.

Biographical details in keywords, please.

The old woman has been saving photographs. Now she's looking for the young man in the photographs with her. At last she finds him. But the one that comes to meet her is an old man.

The refrigerator's over ten years old. It's working again. But a refrigerator that's over ten years old should be replaced.

Down there, at the end of the path, is the little half-timbered house which, from up above, at the beginning of the path, you cannot see.

These shoes have been made so that you can walk in them.

Passers-by don't notice.

Do we know where?

A dog lives in the neighbourhood. A little dog.

The fisherman couldn't have said it. The fisherman is nowhere to be found in the story.

But the conversation is always interrupted.

The painter repeats himself? But every painting is a new painting. And the same motif doesn't remain the same motif. Mornings in morning light, evenings in evening light.

People can also see it differently. And once times have changed, people will see it differently.

There is nowhere to turn around. If you want to get inside, it'd be best to back in.

To walk across the meadows. Fewer pedestrians are allowed to walk across the meadows.

We'll try it again. But we won't say any thing beforehand.

The regulations are as such that you cannot pass if you've got two cigarette lighters.

If we lose, no matter what, we'll trample the grass.

That's how they came, and that's how they left again. Singing, women and men standing in an open truck. With a red and white flag.

We didn't have anything else.

The men hadn't been home too long.

Some of the women had other men until their own were standing in front of the door again.

If you'd said something sooner, we wouldn't have to ask so many questions now.

Some apartments have voluntarily been cleared.

It can't be that Auntie hears the murmuring of the lake in the hills. But no, the weather changes and then you can in fact hear the lake murmur.

Preserving jars, there are still preserving jars with preserved cherries.

If your mother only knew.

Do we know how?

*On Monday you know that the week's begun.*

Larry comes in. Ah, from Denver. No, from Dallas.

Go on and tear up the photo. There are others.

Here, in this room, there's always something left over from the sun.

If they looked, passers-by could see it, but they don't.

The windows are dark, which doesn't mean that we're not home.

The owl outside in the branches.

The streets aren't wet. The landscape won't turn white. But it's been snowing since this morning.

You're looking for both the painting and the museum in which it hangs.

On the floor the shadows of invisible people.

One remains standing to stare up at the balcony. A few, more, many remain standing to stare up at the balcony.

He says that in the dream he heard sentences which he tried to write down as soon as he awoke.

The page, however, remains blank.

Then letters show up, unopened. Should you open them now? Leave them alone a little longer?

Along the way he stopped on a stair, preoccupied by a thought. Afterwards, he had to wonder whether he was going up or down.

The past . . . come on, tell me something about today.

They say that all the women in Iceland have a lot of children but not always from the same man.

In the meantime, on the cold rooftops, the snow.

You all haven't been to the East in a long time.

Some quotations are fictitious.

If the fisherman knows something, he can be included.

Show us what you've got.

Now one can see that the off-road vehicle has stopped in the gully.

One minute. Two minutes. Three minutes. Four hours. Five hours. Six days. Seven days. Eight days. Nine weeks. Ten weeks. Eleven months. Twelve months.

Some sentences need a long time before they'll allow themselves to be written.

It was probably the border path, it was definitely the border path, but that was a long time ago.

Once the name Michallek came to mind, stress on the first syllable. Then it came to mind a second time, stress on the second.

As we came around the corner we saw that the apartments had been cleared and all the furniture was out on the street.

The oxen knew the way. It was already growing dark, and everything was moving so slow that the chaussee seemed endless.

We knew nothing and couldn't do a thing. Nothing at all? You're welcome to test us.

Go on and grab it.

Another photograph from back then. Thank you, but who are these people?

Soon the map will not be correct. It still shows the lake which recently dried out.

One can see four women and two men, standing. They're standing on the road to Kansas.

Those who say they can't see a thing can let themselves be shown.

Or you'll have to wait a few more days. That's when the migrating birds will come and you can figure out which ones will continue onward and which ones won't.

Here we're the ones who are registered. The unregistered are not here.

Trains run along the motorway.

Day and night one breathes.

In Dortmund, they know where the stress falls.

Last night the past called.

The product doesn't exist any more. The replacement parts still do.

Those who live at the bottom of the high-rise still can say that they live in the high-rise.

Uncle says so, too. The weather's changing. And then the lake will murmur.

We have some old weapons out in the stall. A wooden club, a scythe, an axe.

The red morning. The friendly squirrel. The old pullover. The white cigarette. The cold glass. The wet ashes. The little key. The dead mouse. The dark bread. The heavy pail. The steep stairwell. The soft ticking. The round button. The thin line.

*On Tuesday you know that there's no going back.*

A small yellow plane's coming closer. It circles above the house. Twice, three times.

Didn't you hear? The doorbell rang.

We've been forgotten, say two forgotten people. Intentionally, one says. I wish it was that, says the other.

Once you've found the exit, the music stops.

Around the clock, the air we breathe is there for all.

To discover something, even when you know it's already been discovered.

Of course we could play better, but our rival won't let us.

The newspaper's sneering again.

It continues to snow, and we're out in the vegetable garden.

Do you all still have the old wheelbarrow? We do. Then you can indeed help yourselves.

Suddenly the train came to a stop, and everyone had to get off. We could see that it had come to a stop in front of the bridge.

By now all our parents are dead.

No one knows who planted the pear tree any longer either.

A slice of white bread, a slice of cheese.

No one wants to hear that name any more. But you can't get rid of it. Which name do you all mean, exactly?

The hour of snow. The day of gooseberries. The week of abstinence. The month of general mobilization.

The list was under the leaves that had blown in through the open window.

But then the steps that were coming closer soon became the steps that were moving away again.

He only had his briefcase.

If one of you is waiting in front of the entrance and the other in front of the exit, you can end up waiting a long time.

Those aren't neighbours, they don't even know each other, they're just standing next to each other alphabetically.

Men arrived in the garrison town. They were wearing hats, bought newspapers.

In the station, everything still ran according to plan.

A narrow wooden footbridge led over the river next to the bridge whose rubble lay in the rushing water.

He doesn't say too much when he talks about the time when no one knew how long they'd be away.

At the Front, the horses stood outside.

Replacement parts? If they came at all, they came too late.

At some point the suitcases were found again. They were empty and their locks had been broken.

Do we know where?

Now the owl has said something, and those who have understood it have also understood how long they still have to live.

We followed the path that wound down into the valley. We stood there for a while. Then we picked up our packs again and followed the path that wound into the woods.

Hello, we won't be here too long.

One recognizes those kinds of faces. Back then they were also those kinds of faces.

One person, himself named Michallek, has already heard the stress on all three syllables.

The fisherman shakes his head. He cannot say which story he appears in.

Up until the war, whenever we ate, one chapter would be read aloud.

It had either continued to snow or melted overnight. In any event, the tracks around the house could no longer be found.

Way up high, on the last branch, a lone crow looks down onto the house.

Dragging the trashcan through the snow.

Some of the objects he touched had already fallen over.

Where does this river flow? Into the next river.

From the white hills one looks down onto the green plains.

Trickle ever thinner. Ever wider the tap.

Sometimes he sits upstairs in the little room which is full of empty suitcases.

One of the notebooks was read out loud once. And yet it hadn't been finished; somewhere in the middle the notes  just stopped. When the reader got to that point, he hesitated, then leafed through the rest, slowly and with great concentration, all the way through to the end.

That's right, you still know a few of the people. You don't hear from them often, but you know that they're still around.

And what kind of traces were they? Did they go into the house, come out of the house, go around the house?

For a long time some of the refugees who'd stayed still referred to themselves as refugees.

*By Wednesday you've gotten used to the whole thing and remember how it all goes.*

Today the sun isn't shining either, and we're eating fried eggs.

You wouldn't always receive the mail. But then you would start receiving the mail again.

The missing are still there. But where?

The river which flows into the next river leaves its name behind.

We don't know any men who still crush stones. Still, there are some men who crush stones.

The off-road vehicle has stopped in front of the opera house.

Down in the green plains one looks up at the white hills.

Suddenly you are standing in a large apartment among a great number of strangers and are totally confused. But you belong to those who were invited.

It's been a long time since you'd offer someone a cigarette when meeting them.

In the hallway here the buckets. Water bucket, a bucket full of sand.

The host himself doesn't know a lot of the guests.

Strange how such a full glass is soon an empty glass again.

Let's go sweep the snow. It is fresh and pure.

Yesterday evening the glass wasn't cleared off the table. That's why, in the morning, it was still there.

In the driving snow standing on a railway platform. They arrive with iced-over roofs, the late trains, the trains from out of the East.

The sun is there but it doesn't matter, by now the pipes are frozen.

One doesn't see the dead birds. One begins to count the hills in the snow.

When no one calls, you finally have some peace and quiet.

The old man who just died must be quite happy about it.

Our illusions were other illusions.

A day which begins with the memory of a blue dress may be the first of warm spring days to come.

Uncle's son says so too. When you hear the lake murmur, it means the weather is changing.

The whole day long you hear the sounds of planes, but you don't see any planes.

You found the museum, but the painting, where is the painting?

Now go on and show us what you can't do.

Presumably one had expected something else. The traces into the house, out of the house and around the house were our own.

Could you please tell our guests what it was like in the Führer's headquarters, for example, in the kitchen where the chefs from the Adlon Hotel would stand?

You can all lie back down. We'll call for you.

It was the next morning when the child crawled out of the chute.

The blackbirds mornings on Machabäerstraße. Although it's been said already, it's going to be said once more.

Tomorrow one knows how it was today.

There is a point in the room where, of late, the floor creaks.

First thing Father would always pull out was the slide rule.

There are also photographs we haven't been shown.

Towers of empty cans. Two, three birches are still standing. Railroad embankment with broom.

Whenever he'd return, he'd immediately begin to look for something.

The spot on the wall. Someone shot themselves in the mouth here.

The stairs in the hallway led up into the apartments and down into the cellar. In the cellar you'd meet people, in the apartments the doors and windows were open.

Going shopping mornings at eight. Few people about. Few stores open yet.

The off-road vehicle is in a car park, which is empty except for a second off-road vehicle.

Hardly ever a visitor who comes with the tram.

There are multiple points in the room where, of late, the floor creaks.

One's known the two names for a long time. But only just now what their relationship was.

Next item of news. You've got to wait till it's seeped through.

You didn't see your neighbour all winter long. Now he's walking around his house.

Every one of the trucks was empty and one didn't know if they were coming or going.

*On Thursday you know you've almost made it.*

When was it then, the most beautiful time?

No one talks about Michallek any more.

You see, that's just how it goes sometimes.

When a correction followed orders, everything was
open again.

The off-road vehicle is fighting its way through the snowstorm.

He gets out. It is still not too late.

But they were, in fact, our people.

We wanted to grow old together, and it's come to that.

You can all come back inside.

The long route of the ants. This morning they reached
the kitchen table.

It's raining, but if you can count the raindrops, not all
that much.

The rooms upstairs are brighter than the rooms downstairs.

He always said it, and everyone heard it too.

The men who would stand in front of the entrance and wait
were photographed.

A kiosk in the landscape. Otherwise not a single kiosk far and wide.

Among many people, to keep repeating a name until someone looks up.

What you see there is a folding-arm awning.

You'll find out if you keep doing what you're doing.

A construction site. People are procrastinating. Why are people procrastinating, yells the developer.

We did count, and nothing was missing.

A bumblebee finds itself in the room. The whole afternoon already.

The old apple tree will be cut down. Otherwise it will fall down on its own.

The developer is procrastinating. He was told why the others were procrastinating.

The hawk is circling.

Grandfather was aware of it too. For though he was hard of hearing, he knew that, when the weather changed, you could hear the murmur of the lake.

Let's not wait for the evening, we're already tired by the afternoon.

You begin to read a book before you notice that you've read it already.

The pack of cigarettes is empty. That's why you open a new pack of cigarettes.

Something is happening out in the yards.

The branches that were dying in winter now are dead.

More moments pass by than you can hold on to.

You can all come back out.

The large heap is dry, you could make a fire, but before you'd get official permission, the rains will be back.

Field-grey: one of childhood's colours.

The window's open, but the bumblebee can't find its way out.

Shoot, go on and shoot already.

The filling-station attendant is confident. He says, People come to fill up, because if they don't, they can't go anywhere.

Is there still enough paper?

There is no such thing as an empty motorway.

Every day, he says, ends with incertitude. You lie down to sleep, and you never know what's going to happen in your dreams.

One comes inside and either says everything all at once or, at first, says nothing at all.

Where were you last night?

The small yellow plane is back, somewhat further away, somewhat higher.

At night you could hear trains. Nights you would always hear trains.

The first tractor out on the fields. Still. Then it begins to make large circles.

Now the bumblebee buzzes out the open door.

Glancing at the clock. One's startled. Or one's not.

The filling-station attendant says, You don't see the fuel, but it's there.

A bit slower getting up the stairs today.

We'll have one more little one, but then we've got to get going.

When Charlie was still here, the neighbour says, Evenings I'd always be entertained. But she doesn't want a new cat.

Preparations for a trip one doesn't want to take at all.

The morning begins cloudless. At midday a few. Cloudless again in the evening.

The woman wants to go drink a beer. The man doesn't want to go drink a beer.

It was nighttime, and there was nothing to see. The next morning they asked around but every one responded, there was nothing to see, it was nighttime.

First of all, you lost, and then, on top of it, you were guilty for losing.

He had refused as long as he could, but in the end he did it.

*Fridays one goes to see how high the grass has grown.*

The hall was full of people. Every person held a piece of paper with a number in their hand.

Where is the off-road vehicle now? Most recently it was fighting its way through the snowstorm, but that was last winter.

There's a chair lying in the grass. Why isn't it upright?

He immediately had the appropriate phrase at hand. Earlier one could only hear him saying that he didn't want to do it.

Outside in front of the window a ball comes soaring up into view. So high you can see it for a moment from the room.

When it was over, every one went outside.

Start over, then you can make new mistakes.

The undertaker talks about how many people never smoked at all.

The trees are green. You can't see a thing any more.

You bought a book. It's the same one you got as a gift. Now both of them are lying on the table, and you don't know which one to read.

Bittercress and the meadow begins to seem as if made of foam.

The painter says to the poet: You can versify anywhere.

A fruit meadow in the nineteenth century. White sheets lying out to dry. Of the four women who lay them out under the trees, only two are left.

The common people. The cute little people. The cute little chicken people.

What did you all talk about the whole time then? The whole time we talked about the sound that does not exist.

Yesterday evening a storm broke in-between.

The beanpoles are almost all the same height. They made it through the whole winter together.

But the first sound one heard as a child is not the first sound that one remembers.

A lot of cars are yellow now.

At night, when it grows cold, you go and grab a sweater.

And after a minute, twelve months had already passed.

All day long a wind blowing the yellow seed dust of the evergreens through the streets.

The departing train. The tree. The fence. The factory chimney. The wheatfield. The riverbank. The row of poplars. The house. The row of poplars. The riverbank. The wheatfield. The factory chimney. The fence. The tree. The departing train.

You know everything so quickly now.

When the weather changed, in order to hear the murmuring of the lake, Grandmother would go to the gate.

Around the wash trough four white sheets on the meadow. The painter didn't change a thing.

In particular, there are stories that haven't been told. Otherwise, there would only be stories that existed already, because they'd been told.

Go and pick me some flowers.

The fly knows. It flies out the window through which it flew inside.

The neighbour drives to the seaside and parks for three days in a car park.

One moves forward, but up front is somewhere else.

One walks to the end of the yard and thinks, There should be a bench here.

When you win, you're also not guilty.

Again a photograph from back then. Thank you, but what does 'back then' mean here.

At the beginning, not everyone took part.

Just go and have a look. You'll see if something is going on.

With this kind of weather we won't be able to get anywhere.

What do you have to say? The one questioned raises his hands. I don't know any more. And tomorrow I've got to be on my way.

That's a young man in the old passport photo there. The one in this new photo here is old.

One goes and then comes back.

The door won't open.

You didn't hear a thing, but the dog raised its head.

The meadow's been freshly cut, and already the blackbirds are hopping around.

*Saturday. Why is it so cold?*

Where just yesterday the row of trees, today the row of houses.

We haven't seen each other in such a long time. We already thought we'd never see each other again.

The house over there is uninhabited, but sometimes there are voices in the yard, and sometimes you can hear a saw.

You have to remember every day.

Once upon a time you actually believed you could sigh.

Do we know when?

Go and wash your hands first.

A light. A re-found note. A trusty sweater. A screw that fits. A mild type of coffee. A rain gutter that's been fixed. A radio in the background. A bank statement.

The grass had already grown back and before the holidays the price of fuel went sky high. Visitors stood in front of a closed door, and by the time the photographers arrived, it had stopped raining.

Next to the fisherman now a second fisherman. Neither speaks all that much.

Father came home and said, There is no war.

The jukebox was too loud. Someone called the police. One of the officers began to dance. One of the girls shoved a strawberry into his mouth.

Hearing voices again. Once again failing to hear what they're saying.

Hard to tell he waved hello, the man on the tractor.

Cherry trees shortly after the attack.

A number of times a day the notion of different, but simultaneous lives.

He was sitting by the window, and when he raised his head, he could see the sailboats outside on Lake Wannsee. There weren't any sailboats outside, and it wasn't Lake Wannsee.

By the time the young boy walked into the apartment, Mother was already gone.

A new light bulb. If you were one of those Englishmen that are said to exist, you'd be sad about the old one.

Once again, a bit slower going up the stairs.

Letting things come. Letting things go.

The next one has to ask themselves whether they still want to be the next one.

The off-road vehicle has overtaken the tractor.

The passport was expired, but it still looked new.

An assassination attempt. One didn't talk about it. Nor was it investigated. The investigators themselves ensnared in cases that were not investigated.

Fine, if you know everything already.

When it is hot and dry, you don't see any snails in the garden.

What should one do? One does what one can. One does what one can't.

*Motorcycles whining through the village. It's Sunday.*

Watching TV for hours. And then what?

After the storm the sun, immediately humid again, the next storm.

A hissing. Gravel sliding off the loading bed.

He says, Night's shorter when you can sleep.

Yesterday we closed the windows, and today it's cold.

What's so-and-so up to . . . the question about a person whose time is now behind them.

There are visitors who are welcome as long as they stay away.

The milk's been in the refrigerator for a week, but it's still fresh.

Once upon a time a person appeared. She was standing on the Curonian Spit.

Flipped open, welcoming, the lawn chair on the terrace. Welcoming someone to sit.

At night the man would sleep in his tent, hidden in the woods; during the day he'd go eat soup and pick up his mail.

Before flying off, the woodpecker lets himself drop.

It is hot and damp, and out in the garden there are snails.

The day hasn't ended yet, and you don't know what's still to come.

Flags hanging from the windows. That hasn't happened in a long time, and he almost got scared. Not all windows have flags. But some of them do.

The filling-station attendant says, Air doesn't cost a thing, air is priceless.

Cloudless the night. You should be able to see the stars. If you can't see any stars, the night isn't cloudless.

The boy had come along to the station and waved after the train. He didn't realize how soon he would be sitting on the same train himself.

It's the same house, but the people living there today don't know it.

After that, he began to count the days. At some point, it became too much, so he began to count the months instead. Years.

Were they civilians, or did they look like civilians?

Get on with it.

The house isn't really new, but it doesn't have a coal cellar.

Even in the dark you could locate the targets.

Old women wearing bright clothing and going to the cemetery in the mornings.

We didn't dare to call any more. In the end, we only got the answering machine.

Being there but unable to stop this long taking-leave from being.

You sit until you just have to get up and go.

Even before receiving news of their death, the memories.

In the past, not having any thing, you could not lose any thing either.

How does it look over in the East? We haven't been in the East for a long time. Is there a reason?

When there's a hornet in the room you act differently than when there's a bumblebee.

A red plane comes into view, and one places one's hands above one's eyes.

Briefcase, papers, keys, everything in the jacket someone
had lent you in your dream, someone who keeps falling
further and further away.

What do you expect? For years you were silent,
and now you're surprised at being asked why you
were silent for years.

There was a time we stood on the banks of the Oder and
watched the drift ice. Once it was dark and you couldn't
see a thing, we could hear the drift ice.

*The pea field. On Monday we are going to the pea field.*

When he awoke, everything came back to him.

Do we know why?

That's how things began in the war, with a few roof tiles.

The letter has been lying there for a week. For a week
the letter has been lying there.

The white walls are supposed to be painted white. The
painters come and begin. The white walls get painted white.

How long an instant can stretch.

The man has flown to Berlin. As soon as he lands, he calls
home. The woman is still cleaning up after breakfast.

The disadvantage to his sudden fame is that he can no
longer go into town. What should he do instead. He goes
into town anyway.

The mail carrier pedals by.

At the beginning, it was risky; later, one got used to it.

The orchestra consisted of three orchestral units, in the shape of a horseshoe. The first was directed by Pierre Boulez.

Journal Two

Inside the wardrobe there was another wardrobe, but not everyone knew about it.

Now even the grandchild talks about it. When you can hear the murmuring of the lake, up there in the hills, the weather is changing.

Sometimes we'd be called over to the neighbours'. They had a telephone. It hung on the wall in the hall.

The furniture just stands there as if nothing happened.

Be seeing you.

To be prepared for the worst, he always imagined the worst.

Think about tomorrow. Making marmalade.

In the room next door, maybe they know more.

You just have to wait a bit, then you can find the new releases in the used bookstores.

Already packing suitcases again. Father kept a suitcase in the closet; it was always packed.

One hasn't seen the off-road vehicle for a long time.
It was in the barn. Now it is in front of the barn.

Travelling you see butterflies that you don't see back home.

Was there a fire here? The meadows look burnt.
There was no fire here.

Cows lying in the shade of the poplars.

The approaching storm reminds one of the way the
Front approached.

*Tuesday. The storm did not come any closer. It moved on.*

A lovely evening, cool breeze coming off the sea, and we walked across the car park to where they were grilling sausages.

A neighbour stayed home. In the evenings she makes her way through the neighbourhood with her watering can, watering the tomatoes.

The children have school holidays. The grown-ups take holidays.

At night all the windows are open. During the day the rooms are darkened.

The coastal painter has moved inland. The swimmers have arrived. He can only paint when the coast is empty.

Once, when it was raining, it rained so little that the drops on the street were already dry before the next ones came.

If everyone is gone, then no one is left.

Baltic Sea, written on an old English map.

Millions of apples ripening in the gardens nearby.

In the afternoons the clinking of silverware from all the yards.

And if this relentless heat continues, the ice-cream man sighs.

At daybreak we stepped onto the tarmac and walked past the American president's plane.

Strawberry fields all the way to the horizon.

Finding the right connection depends on the right buttons.

A boat with a blue light, racing along the coast.

What a relief not to see the sun for once.

What is this fish called?

The letterbox is in the bushes. The key is hanging in the adjoining tree, on a withered white branch.

He says he only sweats because he's hot.

No one bothers looking for the painter any more, the one who disappeared into the woods right after the war. Recently someone wanted to know about him, but then they disappeared too. No one looked; he was imaginary.

Between 6 p.m. and 6 a.m. there's the danger of running into game.

Passing houses one would like to own and be able to visit twice a year.

Describe a dune. That'll take too long.

If a thatched roof catches fire, the arsonist knows how impressive he'll seem to the firemen.

A person from the Rhineland comes and tells a joke right away: Here I am in a foreign country, and yet I can still understand the language.

The boat comes back, drifts along the beach, this time without the blue light.

Tufts of grass across the dunes. They look dry, but you can see them growing.

The two bunkers have been down by the water forever. Earlier they were further up shore. But that was it. Later on, the watchtower. Now that's gone too.

The two pens are lying next to each other on the table. They are almost the same; both are made by Faber-Castell. Both are green. One is light green, the other dark.

The winter barley is flowering everywhere. But if it's been dry a long time, the harvest is thin.

In the West you have no idea what they think in the East.

Some of the visitors here stop in the Tyrol in-between.

Filling the rain barrel with tap water.

You can think yourself away without having to think of a way back.

We wanted to go to Trinwillershagen tomorrow, but will only be able to make it the day after.

Someone had kept a bunch of postcards: their parents on summer holidays, Strength Through Joy, photographs of sandcastles, steamboats, hotels.

Shower rooms are rooms where one can clean oneself from head to toe.

The blue of the Nivea tin.

A brief commemoration. Then everyone went back to their own living rooms.

The rooms downstairs are high ceilinged and huge. The rooms upstairs are low ceilinged and tiny. The rooms in between are either more cramped and tinier or even more spacious and massive.

So who were you when you were wearing a uniform? Warrant Officer Class Two. And what are you doing here now? Turning off the light.

He said, In the evenings I like to take the old ways, but the truth is no longer true.

The filling-station attendant knew the area perfectly. Or, in any event, he says, like it used to be.

Hello. Where are you calling from?

The *Wehrmacht* had ceased to exist, but we continued to sleep in its tents.

It is your name and it is your handwriting.

You yourself the time which passes so quickly.

The attacker complaining that he was the one attacked.

The people from upstairs now live downstairs.

During the night we could hear the marten under the eaves. In the morning the decapitated head of a marten in front of the door.

We're arriving so late because we spent too long going the wrong way.

Can you grab a snail without pausing first?

He has finally broken his silence. What do you mean? He was never silent.

Everyone, before sitting down, looked below their seat.

Thirty years later he called once more. He said, Maybe it wasn't right.

There are a few stones on the table. They had been lying where all the small stones lie, on the beach.

To figure out what it is that makes one so anxious the whole day long, but one doesn't.

Quiet the evening through till dawn.

The letter had been there a few days. But now the letter is gone.

One saw him occasionally, the tenant, a polite, unremarkable young man, and now they say that he disappeared overnight.

We have a cook, a gardener, a tailor, and we are seeking a carpenter, a tiler, an electrician, a bus driver, a crane operator, a secretary.

How one would look for a fight, find their enemy and not need a war at all.

By the time someone yelled, Stop! it was already too late.

Looking out front, you see that it's raining. Looking out back, you don't see any rain at all.

Not all the people who are not there have gone on a trip.

The village has been cleared.

They didn't stay very long. And why should they have?

We're not going to hurt you.

You can't always sleep, and during the day you don't have a lot of time.

*On Wednesday afternoons, it is quiet in the suburbs. Many of the smaller stores are closed.*

Don't leave the ladder outside at night.

We didn't know the man at the table. But he brought up names, names from the past, which we alone thought we recognized. In the end, he knew our names too.

Afternoon. Since this morning the sound of two mechanical saws in the distance. Like a kind of race.

The man at the table, then he brought up names we didn't know. We were amazed by how many names, all the names he kept bringing up. Now and again closing his eyes as if reading from a list somewhere deep inside himself.

Five storms in a single day. In the evening the sixth.

Please shut the door.

The sun was shining by the time the off-road vehicle finally rolled back into the farmyard, shortly before the sixth storm.

Nothing is ever going on. Today there is too much going on.

One drove to a hotel in the countryside, thinking that it would be a quiet place. It wasn't a quiet place.

There are people who have to get up multiple times a day to walk out of their offices and stand in the fresh air, in front of the door.

It's growing dark. That's why we've gotten up and are making our way to the light switch.

Plop. A bird has flown into the windowpane.

In the early morning the telephone. One hardly finds the nerve to pick it up.

Can you say what you are thinking at any given moment?

Most of the time you cannot smell a thing, for there is nothing in particular to smell.

A coffee machine full of coffee. Now you just need a cup.

In the past, he fell out of his bed a few times.

Today, making his way across the meadow, he was over-taken by a bumblebee.

When you've lent someone your bicycle you cannot say where, at the moment, it is.

In the garden, in a small patch, the potatoes. Although we know you can buy them.

The filling-station attendant knows why, at weekends, the client brings an empty canister.

The neighbour needs a stamp for his chicken eggs. He does not have a stamp.

Soon, she said then asked, When is soon?

If you feel something soft underfoot, it might be a plum.

It won't work without it.

The voice from a time one spoke more slowly.

His childhood was a school of silence. Perhaps, he says, that is the reason why he has never been able to really tell a story.

An old habit, hammering crooked nails straight.

One didn't notice a thing, for years not a thing. But then it began and one was surprised that one hadn't noticed a thing for years.

There is nothing in the paper about it. One was waiting for something to be in the paper.

Without a doubt it was meant differently, but at this point that doesn't help at all.

You have no idea what has changed. And we're not too sure either.

After a long time, another postcard arrives. Otherwise everything's the same as always.

Down in the meadow. The last of the old pear trees. Just a few pears. High up in the branches.

In October large and beautiful cloudscapes pushed from west to east.

Are we waiting again already? Or did we forget that we hadn't stopped?

He leant against the windowsill. Felt as if it were two storeys below.

Can anyone tell you how long you still have to live?

In the past, one listened for the owl, and when you heard it, you'd look at each other.

Then we had a telephone ourselves, it stood on the table in the corner.

The light flickering all night. Once we turned it off, it never came back on.

Where is the piece of paper? The small, red one, the one with two words.

Slept soundly. During the night the clock went back an hour.

The apples which had been hanging next to one another in the tree are now lying next to one another in the grass.

The wheelbarrow you're pushing can also be pulled.

After funerals, the old ones meet on their birthdays.

A trace of oil. The off-road vehicle is losing oil.

You all are never at home. Whenever we call, you are never at home.

It was dark already by the time the man with the hedge-clippers came.

At the end of October the mice return to the house.

Pulling the trashcan through the sand.

Calling an office that at the same time is calling other offices.

A friend returns from Greece and says, It was so lovely when it rained.

The radio announcer reads an announcement which is five minutes long and thirty-one years old.

By the end of the war three years old, but that's old enough to be a witness.

*Wednesday still? No, Thursday, for a long time already now.*

Then you know what's coming. You don't?

Another construction site. This time it's a canal. The construction firm said that the access road would be blocked for two weeks. It's been three weeks already.

The neighbourhood cat now sleeps behind the trashcan. She doesn't want to go back home. There's got to be a reason.

The cows still spend the nights outside, and mornings in the fog.

When the wind blows, a rose you don't see when it's still bobs up and down in front of the kitchen window.

In the evenings one can sit and do something which is nothing.

He said, If nothing occurs to you, just numbering the next pages is already a step forward.

He said, I don't smoke any more, here and there I just light a cigarette.

Yesterday we did something wrong, but we only realize that today.

What one doesn't want to believe when one sees leaves on the meadow.

The deer you saw jump across the rural road was a buck.

The no-longer-so-young woman, who has already had to look for a new job multiple times, is now working at a funeral home. She is happy because it looks like she has found a secure spot.

Still enough water.

The train departed on time. But whether it will arrive on time is another question.

Getting up at night. But if what you were dreaming has not yet come to an end, it is better to lie back down.

When he said that the sun was so low that you couldn't see it, he was asked what he meant.

Everyone is inside, and one cannot see what they are doing.

Fog. A man walking. Walking in fog.

A thin, grey, crinkled line across the paper. A thin, grey, crinkled strand of hair.

Two letters got crossed in the mail. As the one letter knows nothing of the other, a complication arose. If the two letter writers ask for an explanation, there is the risk that the letters will again get crossed.

How did the nail get into the off-road vehicle's tyre? One asks because one doesn't know.

In the early morning a red strip of sky across the ridge, and we talk about how the December light appears in the bedroom window.

In the red of evening sky, red condensation trails moving westward.

The middle of December and by the time we pick the last apples, the hard green Ontarios, from the tree, still no snow. Climbing plants at our feet, wet, yellow weeds hiding the beauty of the rampant nasturtium. Night frost in November, and the crops are destroyed.

Winter: sitting in the chair in front of the table for longer than usual.

To go and get wood from the shed, where it's already dark, before it's dark.

During the night he got up a few times and walked through the house. When he saw that he had left the light on somewhere, he turned it off as he passed.

Sometimes, even when everything is there, one feels as if something were missing.

Have a look outside again.

The neighbour, who was walking around his house, is now going back inside.

Since when has the painting been crooked? Just a bit ago it was straight. But when was that?

When mail would arrive from someone who had died.

Once it had gotten a little warm, the small stove shut itself off.

The road we took into the valley yesterday is closed today.

At the inn, which we'd found in the dark, everything was dark.

The filling-station attendant can't say how the nail got into the tyre either. He says, But I can repair it.

In the cemetery the tombstone with the engraved dates of the dead, which the mason drew and drew while the dying one slept.

Customs stop on the motorway. It has begun to snow. Are we from one of the countries in the east?

The architect's sky is crooked. The minister's garden wants to connect. The lawyer's woods make no exceptions.

Rest stops, motels, filling stations; you never have to leave the motorway.

While it continued to snow, we would carry the Christmas tree out of the woods, in the twilight, before the sirens began to howl.

It was growing dark when he left the house for a walk.

Here and there a few more cigarettes, but still a few less.

Perhaps, the old man says, everything will still change.

In the evenings, around six o'clock, the sound of bells.

The farm. The broom. A dog. A handcart.

Growing older he looked into the mirror evermore seldom, looking evermore like his father.

A winter sky between two bare branches. A pale, eastern light on the western plain.

The pinewoods. The sandy paths along the motorway. The blank old postcard. The capital of the Reich.

One drives into town in the right-hand lane. One drives out of town in the left-hand lane.

*It's still Thursday, as it has been for a while. Sometimes we live more slowly, sometimes more quickly.*

My whole life, the old woman says, I have had to look for things, from my glasses to my keys, my passport to my tickets. But I have never lost a thing.

If we stay on the motorway, we'll get home.

He said that he found himself beyond what had been achieved and what hadn't.

The *blitzkrieg* has wandered off with *cosiness*. *Weltanschauung* has gone missing, with *angst* behind it. The *zeitgeist* emigrated a long time ago, and the *coffee klatch* isn't there any more either.

In the past he often used to stand at the bar. He no longer stands at the bar.

Most of the time the two friends whose wives have died sit at home.

In the past the infantry would march down the rural road. Now they drive down the motorway.

Do you still have the old tent?

Then we were standing by the river and looking into a foreign country.

Railway tracks in between which birch.

Pass me the map.

We've got to ask.

One drives out of town in the right-hand lane. One drives into town in the left-hand lane.

Early in the morning a friend calls. She says, Go out and get a copy of today's paper.

He realizes he should 'move' more often. Not only from room to room, or through the garage or across the street to this or that pub, and regardless of whether he's in the East or the West.

So, you were at the cinema.

We sat and smoked. (Hemingway.)

He lay down to nap in the afternoon. When he woke, it was dark and evening already. The headlights of a passing car wandered across the ceiling. He thought he was back in his childhood where, when he was sent to bed early, he would count the passing cars. After the first, it took a while before he heard a second car, a third. Each with its lights off.

Every street had a name that remained its name, as if it had been one's own. Every one of the biographical streets.

Whenever you meet someone who happened to live on the same street, even when you don't know them, it's like they're a confidant, an accomplice, an insider.

In almost every house a secret, hidden story.

Distant voices although those talking are sitting
at the same table.

The one sleeping is woken. He feels as if he hadn't slept
at all.

Those who do not wake are not asleep either.

People come in to the room where one had gone to escape.

At night, lying awake, a phrase had come, which, by the next morning, had disappeared again.

Why doesn't the light in the stairwell work?

The apartment is empty, but the mail carrier continues to deliver the mail.

Another former colleague buried. Parakeets in the trees. See you next time. Do make sure you come to the summer party.

At night, cars parked halfway onto the pavement, halfway onto the street.

The pencil is lying on the table. The table is in the room next door.

If you wear a black shirt, you are already considered a fascist.

*In the past, you only ate fish on Fridays. Today is Friday, and there is no fish.*

The off-road vehicle exploded. The off-road vehicle in the news.

He saw the tram passing through the woods.

Talking about snow, as if it were something that only appeared in fairy tales.

People said it was a miracle that nothing else happened.

No one ever came to take anyone from our neighbourhood away.

Let the roller blinds down.

Yesterday we saw a man running after another man.

This photograph, the photographer says, was waiting
for me to take it.

We had grown so accustomed to the debris that we missed
it once it was gone.

A cat comes to visit. The following day she comes again.

Strawberries in January.

He sat before his teacup and stirred in it with his spoon.
He looked like he would never stop stirring.

Go on and raise the roller blinds.

So, what was in today's paper?

Crossing the street he stumbled and fell. His two young
companions helped him to his feet. Everything's OK. You're
OK? He grumbled for a while. For it had to have been
something with his sense of orientation that caused him
to stumble.

The two tall pear trees fell with the last storm. They were
old, dead and dried out. We'd left them standing, but can
we leave them lying?

What happened to the two fishermen? A little while ago
they were still there.

No more trains; more grass and undergrowth on the trestle.

A man was lying on the side of the rural road. We stopped and got out. When we bent over him he raised his head and asked: What's wrong?

The inn which had been in the dark is now in the light.

Four-hour winter.

The gardener is out in the meadow counting the trees which are no longer there.

Living in the country, living in the city. Not being able to do both at once, you have to drive back and forth.

In the past, not everyone had a bicycle. Even today not everyone has a bicycle.

The photo shows four men sitting around a table. But there were eight men.

We expect the rain to stay outside.

The cat jumps onto the bed.

We are sitting close to the oven because it is warm.

It won't stop raining. The puddles are growing larger and coming closer to the house. Puddles surround the house.

If it's the marten, it got into the house at night.

What do you see now? Black branches against a clear sky.

There isn't any wind? There is wind.

The road into the valley, which was closed, is open again.

There is always a light on in the hotel.

The church is older.

People think, the filling-station attendant says, that I don't have any thing to do when no one's here.

In the past, there was a post office here, and the person who sold stamps was a post-office clerk. Now you stand in line at the supermarket and buy your stamps from a part-time worker.

Waiting rooms are for sitting and waiting. There are never any empty waiting rooms. The people who are waiting look healthy, but they are all ill.

If that were the case, then you would have to think about who you would like to see one more time.

The cat, which jumped onto the bed, is lying on the bed.

On every street corner there was a guard.

Does the second sip taste any different than the first?

*In the West weekends begin on Saturday, in the East on the evening before Sunday.*

A fisherman. One of the two who have disappeared or a third?

When sitting he places his right hand over his left. After a while, he places his left hand over his right.

As there were no chairs, everyone had to stand.

Afternoon sun. Arrives unexpectedly. Doesn't stay long. It blinds drivers. Yellow crocuses. The blackbird's yellow beak.

Inside the inn which is in the light it still is dark.

One mentions a couple of names and thinks, Everyone knows them. They were really well-known names.

Don't smoke so much (Handke.)

He said, It's almost certain that I won't come, but I still want to be invited.

Evenings he goes out with the empty canister to the stable. When he returns, the canister is full. The canister is full of oil. The oil is kept in an oil tank. The oil tank is in the stable and has a pump. The pump is there so that you can pump oil from the tank into the canister.

Sometimes there is a nod of recognition, sometimes a disapproving shake of the head, sometimes a condescending laugh. It has to do with the brand of off-road vehicle.

There are some people you don't want to have anything to do with.

We are now prepared, says the county commissioner, we now have the proper structures.

On the other hand, there are some people you will never understand.

Do you get how it works now? Yes, but only in winter.

The filling-station attendant says, The filling station is there for every kind of car.

The air smells on snow, and it looks like it will snow any minute, but, by evening, it still hasn't snowed.

Sometimes the old people one dreams about in the dream are young.

He made a sketch. Very carefully. Why so carefully? After the sketch you'll keep going. No, after the sketch I won't keep going.

You've heard the good news, we lost.

The bombers would arrive around noon. They would not stay long.

Snow-free slopes. Ice-free harbours.

Yesterday evening a man talked about how he had seen three boards in the river. First one, then the other, then the other. After the third, the man said, he didn't see any more.

Does one receive more the second time round?

When Father grew suspicious, he knew why.

In the meantime, we went into the room next door and got the pencil which was lying on the table.

Most of the time one knows what caused one to stumble.

One can see that the swans are white, and are flying.

Tomorrow today's paper is no longer available.

The fisherman is a third fisherman.

The flowers in the vase. They should be given water
and placed out in the cold at night.

To do something secretly. To finish off the chocolate.

You're not thirsty, but you are supposed to drink
the whole day long.

What is the kitchen knife doing in the bedroom?

At night the whole house is cold.

The woman, the one who found a secure position at the
funeral home, says, We have seven hundred burials a year.

Once we stood on the shadow of a man who was standing
in front of us. But he didn't say any thing and continued
to stand there.

Perhaps you could recognize him because of the way he
folded the newspaper.

Even after the war, the old woman says, her mother continued to work as a tram conductor. She never got to know her
father, but she knows that her mother got to know him in
the tram, he was handsome, in a black uniform.

One kept the windows closed for as long as one could see smoke going into the air.

There were poppies in the grain fields, and we took shelter in the furrows.

Is the second evening as lovely as the first?

After she had said that there we songs one could once again sing along to, she was asked what kind of songs they were.

There is laundry hanging on the neighbour's clothesline. Handtowels, tablecloths, sheets. When the frost comes they will turn as hard as boards.

In the photo one can see people sitting in front of the radio. It's impossible to know what they are listening to, but they have serious faces.

On the table there is an onion. We bought it together with other onions. They all come from New Zealand.

The doorbell. There was a man outside. He immediately began to talk about his life.

She said she loves to sing the song 'Im Märzen der Bauer sein Rößlein einspannt'. But she can only sing it in March.

*Sundays he did not feel well when in the morning he had to put on his Sunday suit and keep it on the whole day long.*

What does the empty carton in the middle of the living room mean?

Now and then we would go to the window and look up and down the street.

Still winter; the meadow doesn't need to be cut.

You go to the barber. Two men are waiting. One has long hair, the other short.

Which radio station are you listening to there?

For the third fisherman everything is starting from scratch.

If smokers die sooner, then non-smokers die later.

During the war, the old man says, we didn't go down to the cellar every day either.

Does one get married a second time because one is older than the first time around?

If you don't want to drive one, you don't have to have an off-road vehicle.

Today the vegetable soup tastes just as good as it did yesterday. To be honest, even better.

Some of what he said sounded absurd. But he wasn't saying any thing absurd.

It does not look as if the snowdrops need any sun. But now it's there, and the snowdrops are blooming.

Magpies and crows hopping about the meadow. The crows are hopping on to the magpies.

A driver stops and asks the way to Olpe. Which Olpe, the filling-station attendant asks, we have two. The driver doesn't know. Then take the rural road here to the one, and if that's not it, then take the motorway there to the other.

There are villages here where the people have the same names.

There were two clocks in the kitchen. One was ahead, the other was behind.

Even the smallest houses had a garden, a stable.

When the woods were larger, it was colder.

Children would be led across the street, in long rows of three. Being led to church.

In the morning he ate his first apple, in the evening the last.

If you clean the table now, you have to know that you'll soon be cleaning the table again.

For long-distance targets there were rockets.

But there were the Paffraths in Herkenrath, the Herkenraths in Paffrath, the Kürtens in Odenthal and the Odenthals in Kürten.

As he didn't know what to do in the afternoon, in the afternoon he did little of anything.

And then? Then we turned off the radio, got up and went outside to get some fresh air.

They wanted to know the truth. We kept to our story and said, The vegetable soup tastes even better today than it did yesterday.

We thought it had grown late, and it had, in fact, grown late.

The tram to come. The summer to come. The defeat to come. The reunion to come. The confusion to come. The unreal to come. The letter to come. The street to come. The lapse to come. The life to come. The morning to come.

The excavator is there. Why?

A single chair was left in the room, as if to say, the room is empty now.

Hello. Do you know how to drive an omnibus?

A young man flies to Algeria to walk through the desert.

A letter arrives, but this is not the right address. You have to go out to the street and to the letterbox to send it back on its way, back to the right address.

One sees two men. One of them is walking to the letterbox, the other walking away.

The one says how it was. The other says that's not how it was.

Why does the matchbox have only burnt matches?

Lying down with his eyes closed he could hear the murmuring. With his eyes open, he couldn't.

It is windy. It is dark. It is cold.

Every day there is war.

Both women were wearing clothes that reached to their feet. They were taking the path across the fields to Refrath.

He had introduced himself as Riding Master Düvelius, and you could see it, even though he was not in uniform.

How was the night?

He didn't talk about it, and one couldn't see that he was ill.

Now one has also forgotten that one had forgotten the key.

Tomorrow the day can be very long. The day after tomorrow can be very short.

Before leaving the room, he took one more look around. He noticed that the cup he had looked for in the kitchen was on the windowsill.

You used to receive the answer first, then the question.

Along the way to the hospital you could see the first white magnolia blossoms.

*Monday was supposed to be a short day. It turned into a long one.*

You heard things that you did not want to hear at all.

Good evening. Would you care for a roll or a slice of bread with breakfast?

Memory's sigh. Please, no more impressions.

Once the carpenter said, You can nail screws, but you cannot screw nails.

If they show remorse, the old culprits, they can return home.

Little movement. With movement, the burden of the body must be moved with.

Does the second time have the same cause as the first?

Now it is happening on TV: the front is approaching.

Again one would have to name names. They would be the same names. There aren't any others.

Finally night arrived. Finally morning arrived.

Coming out of anaesthesia, he immediately tried to stand up. Numerous times. Later they told him that they had kept him from doing so.

The inventor, whose inventions no one understands, is the dream.

It is still light, but there are rooms where the lights are coming on.

One does not hear a thing from him, and he doesn't show himself either. One only knows that he has not given up.

Occasionally, but so that no one notices, one says to oneself, Nothing helps.

Then there is a vase full of poppies on the table, and the poppies come from Iceland.

Does one know any other names? Of course, but one only names the names one always does.

He called us his friends, and we acted like we were his friends.

You know what will happen if you don't stop.

A while already, out on the terrace.

*It was a Tuesday morning when suddenly a crane appeared in the middle of the garden, its arm moving back and forth the whole day long.*

Stepping into a room and immediately moving to open the window.

There are no poppies that come from Iceland.

A rediscovered photograph. Your sister is wearing a summer dress, your brother a winter uniform.

Once he stood in front of a closed level crossing which, though no train had passed, went back up after fifteen minutes.

The taste of frozen potatoes.

One sees the off-road vehicle standing on the forest path. It is standing there because it is waiting for the toads to pass.

At night we could hear the night fighters returning.

There were only a few.

A friend says that she flies to far away islands in order
to read.

The table has been set for eight people, but there are
nine standing around it.

Once again rubbing one's hands together. One has discovered that the past of a meritorious man is not without flaw.

An old map has resurfaced. Someone had drawn a blue line,
a boundary line.

After looking at the pictures, for a while it was quiet.

No one is to know he was in the hospital. He was not in
the hospital for a long time.

The sky is cloudless, and one can see how many planes,
high up and silent, are passing.

One stood in the doorway and saw the car that they had
been waiting for come round the corner.

Can you peel strawberries?

What makes a day long, what makes a day short?

Why doesn't your name come up any more?

The one can do it. The other cannot.

On the eighteenth floor a man walked onto the balcony.

He smoked, held a glass in his hand and looked out over the city.

We've got to go back. We forgot the oranges.

Come on. Let's tolerate one another again.

Once we saw a train stopped on one of the abandoned tracks. It consisted of sleeping cars. Not a single door was opened, and all the curtains were drawn.

In the morning a call from the district savings bank, in the afternoon from the Döberitzer Heath.

Future generations know it from future generations.

A train station appears in the course of everyone's life.

In the afternoon one left the building one had entered in the morning.

When you have a garden, you know you've got work to do.

Did we know, as children, what childhood was?

He sighs when he is asked what he doesn't want to speak about.

A man puts down a suitcase and walks on. One must know that the man, having returned from a trip, is in his apartment.

*On Wednesday the crane was no longer there.*

The first walkers in the morning have dogs. In the mornings the first dogs with their walkers.

Looking for an interview. The interviewer is no longer alive. The interviewee doesn't know any more. The interview no longer exists.

The cuckoo flies alone. One doesn't see it return.
It comes at night.

A suburban side street. The only people who know about it are the people who live there.

One sees two cars avoid each other. Otherwise one would see them crash.

An ill woman calls. She calls to talk about her illness.

For a time he would collect the shrapnel from anti-aircraft shells. Until the anti-aircraft guns ceased firing.

The young man walking through the desert had brought photos of men walking through the desert.

The sun went down. The ship went down. The Reich went down.

One took the door off its hinges. The room looks larger.

The cat was most recently lying on the bed.

An ill man is called. He does not say that he is ill.

An empty metal box on the table. We could use it to store all the odds and ends that are on the table. It is a shimmering silver and seems so perfect that we decide to leave it empty.

Watching someone in the tram filling out a questionnaire.

Sitting in front of a window through which one sees trains passing by, between buildingsides and courtyards. Some hours earlier, sitting in one of the passing trains, one looked up at the windows.

On the phone one says one doesn't know what will happen later on in the evening, who one will meet, what one will say.

This winter, a friend says, Lake Wannsee won't freeze.

Many people meeting in a hall. One can tell many languages are being spoken.

Those who emigrate are asked what their background is.

Though he came down the stairs as quietly as possible, one could hear that he was coming down the stairs.

Those who are fleeing look different.

One knows the places but not the names they now have.

Emptied classrooms, straw mattresses.

A few have gone outside and are standing under the trees.

So what do people who are fleeing look like?

In the dark one can see a few lights on the opposite shore.

He says what he always says, namely, that he could imagine living in one of the old villas.

The following morning no one was left.

In the courtyard everyone is standing together again.
It was not everyone.

That is not our suitcase.

The last toad managed to cross the path. The off-road vehicle can continue.

Only seldom does Father talk about his father.

Lovely weather, terrible mood.

Visitors stop by and ask how one is doing. One says that one is doing well.

The cat is in front of the door. Which means she wants to go outside. The door is opened. The cat sits in the open door.

You should come and try something. One asks oneself why.

Watching a cyclist trying to get on their bicycle. Loaded down with luggage.

Stepping on to an escalator that does not begin to move once it has been stepped upon.

*Thursday one's favourite pub was closed. So one went a block further down.*

Seeing the moon in the afternoon.

One cannot talk to the fisherman. He is standing on the opposite shore.

For a long time he couldn't find reverse. Whenever he thought he'd found it, the car moved a bit forward instead.

The voice from the car radio said, The bird sings with its fingers.

Men in bright orange dungarees pulling branches across the road, right before twilight.

One reads that smoking can be fatal. But one is not given to read that smoking does not have to be fatal.

Sometimes the situation is such that one tries to use an excuse.

This morning a woman says that, in the evening, she is going to beat up a man.

When a relegated team is facing a promoted team, you know you are in the second division.

Before getting up, he emptied the cup in one go.

For the one group it was the way up; for the others, the way down.

To stay in the middle, to find a home.

It was late at night when the small woman let loose on the large man. The fact that he had longer arms did not help either.

Whatever one says in front of the camera does not have to be voluntary.

In the hall where his friends were in the audience, the large man showed up in an armoured car.

All the dirt that gets thrown up by moles consists of innumerable tiny crumbs.

Living with someone else in a house creates more noise than when one lives alone.

Spring. The heat needs to be turned on.

New apples. What to do with the old ones. Beautiful women, who will take the ugly ones.

Two men meet each other. There is a mirror in the room.

Eating at home is cheaper.

Time to plant, the garden centre says. Even in December.

Afterwards, one is always sorry.

The off-road vehicle has received a little brother.

There was always something to eat.

All of a sudden, between the two tanks firing at each other, a small Opel.

The trains were no longer running. Once they began to run again, they stopped before the bridges which were down in the water.

A blank, empty sky, and we buy a green carpet.

To level off the bomb crater, seed it with grass; after one hundred years, a pear tree.

It sounded like the night fighters were roaring right above the house. But the roaring would not stop. It was the wind.

The hostages ask for the troops to be removed. The troops are not removed.

When a car is standing still, the filling-station attendant says, it doesn't use any fuel. If the car is standing still, it could be out of fuel.

Now they are looking for the woman who fell out of the small Opel.

Once the fisherman raised his arm. Would he wave? He moved his arm, and it looked like he was waving.

*When a Friday was Good Friday, the Protestants would go to church and then dig up the Catholics' gardens.*

Wherever there was a tree, for a long time you don't plant another tree.

The weed for the lungs, the key for heaven.

We will only look for the targets for you.

One saw those who never said a word.

Please come inside. Then you can have a look outside.

The prisoners say, We have made a mistake. That is why we are prisoners.

In the afternoon the man and woman drive to the Baltic.

In the dream looking for the car which one had parked in the foreign city.

One has four grandparents.

The newspaper is on the floor. If you don't bend down to pick it up, it will stay there.

Most of what he reads he immediately forgets.

An old woman gets in touch. She saw the photograph in the paper. She says, The young woman who fell out of the Opel is my sister.

In the south a poor harvest; in the north a bit better.

Father's worries. One only understands them later.

Children letting eggs roll down the bushes. Whoever's egg is the first to reach the bottom, gets all the others.

Tell us what you all have made.

The prisoners were let go. They say, Thank you for
the hospitality.

The plane leaving behind a condensation trail, high up in
the sky, is moving ahead of its condensation trail.

She arrived from the road, bringing horse manure.

One lies down in the sun at noon. It is now warm enough
for one to lie in the sun at noon.

Whenever he sat at his desk, he allowed himself a cigarette.
He often sat at his desk.

There is a bicycle race on TV. Every now and then the
cyclists disappear in a tunnel. Then you don't see them
either.

Noise coming through the walls. Otherwise the room
is quiet.

He only wants to know how much more time he has.

One pound of butter, you can weigh it, it's one pound
of butter.

Behind the woods we know begin the woods we don't.

A mouthful of hope. A slice of friendship. A finger's length
of tenderness. A cap of sleep. A handful of silence.

Guests are coming in the evening. Panic in the morning.

What happens to a mistake no one notices?

A jogging man crosses the street. He came out of the woods and disappears back into the woods.

What do you do first when the doorbell rings at the same time as the telephone?

Flakes of snow dancing before the camera. But it's a spring day in Virginia.

The knife grinder asks if we have anything that needs to be sharpened. We have some garden scissors, some nail scissors, some kitchen scissors.

One expected him to follow, but when he didn't follow, one knew that something had happened.

When the sun is on half the table, one closes the shutter. When the sun is on the other half, the other.

Now you are sitting in a darkened room, and outside the sun shines all day long.

Some have to go. Others, however, can stay.

Those who can work must work.

She's got strange eyes. Some people accuse her of possessing the evil eye.

In the past the trashcans were made of metal, and you could fill them with hot ashes.

Cold again. If it stays cold, one will have to go and collect firewood, and turn on the stove.

He said, Let me be, I can do it on my own.

Up the stairs, carefully, like in the old days.

Questions by letter, please. Questions over the phone do not allow you any time to think over the situation in peace.

The rain barrel. It isn't raining.

Planting potatoes, planting beans.

In the morning, bright clouds. In the afternoon, dark clouds.

When it smells of smoke, one opens the window. Or one closes it. It depends on whether the smoke is coming from inside or outside the house.

Two friends have had an argument. Or they say they were friends before the argument.

Now we'll have the salad.

An old acquaintance got in touch. An old story is being warmed up. An old pain makes itself felt.

We call. You all are not there.

In the dream two heads of cauliflower, as big as clouds.

*On Saturdays one goes out into the garden, sits under a parasol and reads the weekend supplement.*

A piece of chalk, an old piece.

In between the rape fields a yellow house.

At first it looked like a comma in the wrong place. Then, when it began to move, one saw that it was a tiny insect.

The filling-station attendant sticks to it. He says, When you can't see the road for the fog, you are seeing the void.

The neighbour lives alone. Now one can hear him telling someone off.

He goes his own way, the off-road vehicle's little brother.

The carpenter is building a new door. Why is it thinner than the old door?

New strife. With new weapons.

The old man who has just died, he wasn't against it either, but for it.

Both have failed. The one says, It depends on the kind of failure. Yes, says the other, up in the first division or down in the second.

Quite right, what's in the newspaper. But if you really want to know, in fact, everything was completely different.

The one must exit, the other can enter.

When someone calls at night, it means that they've already had a few.

He did not measure incorrectly, the carpenter.

The room is used seldom. Why is it such a mess?

Mornings in the market hall. Every thing so cold, so fresh.

Tell me, how do you get rid of inner tension?

Was breakfast good? How was lunch? What was there
to eat for dinner?

Forgetting to water the flowerpots. That can lead to war.

A beer glass out on the meadow. Should it stay there?

You have to get up early if you want to see how empty
the streets are.

Out and about and one starts to look for their house keys.

From time to time he gets tired.

A single watering can is not enough.

One comes and sees a stranger's car parked in front of the
entrance to the garage.

They were indeed our people, no?

A father found his daughter's diary. After reading through it,
he reached for the telephone.

The day began with a T-shirt and a wind from the south,
and ended with a wind from the north and a sweater.

The man is still standing at the bus stop. He lets one bus
after the other pass.

It is a small, ball-shaped wasp's nest that's hanging under the eave in front of the door.

You've baked bread. For the next number of days we have bread.

Holidaymakers returning from the rainy south. The first thing they do is water their parched gardens.

Soon after the war, Father dug a swimming pool in the garden. Whenever friends came over to swim, they brought a few pails of water.

They were definitely our people.

The easiest thing is not to understand any thing any more.

Waking up he no longer knew whom he had wanted to kill in the dream.

Where is one supposed to sit? Too cold in the shade, too warm in the sun.

The beer glass is still out in the meadow.

The small beverage shop is closing. All the people drive to the big beverage shop.

They have not heard from us in a long time. But that does not mean any thing.

Only three out of twelve are left. Not for long. Only one can remain.

Someone has a name which is often confused with someone else with the same name.

A woman is sitting in the courtyard. Resting.

*Sunday. The farmers are gathering hay. Rain has been forecast.*

The village doctor says he doesn't go to the pub because he finds all the people he's written off work for being ill.

The window is open. One can hear someone sweeping, with a hard broom.

Planted a plum tree. As you can see, nothing is going to come of it.

Every time the secretary called, she suggested a different date.

The off-road vehicle wants to know what one intends to do.

Wind in the evening. You only see the green of the trees, how it moves.

Rain was forecast. In the morning one sees that it rained.

The old oil stove kept smoking until it went out and no longer came on.

Our friend the woodpecker has been attacked by an angry titmouse. It's become clear that our friend is a nest robber.

At first it was the father threatening others with the gun, then it was the son.

Occasionally he would go through the house, closing doors.

A taxi drives in to the woods.

There are certain anxieties you can't do any thing about.

It had been brittle for a long time, the handle on the old stall door. Now it has broken off. But that's OK. You can still get the door open, even with the broken-off handle.

One looks through the pocket calendar to find out today's date.

We hadn't been seen for days. Had we gone on a trip?

You run into people that you don't immediately recognize, and then you wonder whether you were recognized yourself.

We sat, surrounded by three orchestras, somewhere in the middle.

The cold marmalade. It stood out in the cold.

You can say what you want, the same thing always comes out.

The old houses which had been completely renovated, many of them are empty now.

Ah, you were over in the East again. How are things over in the East?

Two men meet each other in the empty hotel hall. Are we the first or the last?

What one says when one doesn't know.

Whether you come to the top or the bottom, you have, in any event, reached the end of the stairs.

Driving by seeing people you will never see again.

Drinking Wörlitzer beer in Wörlitz, but it's not actually made in Wörlitz.

A few people have gone outside. It is raining. They are standing in the rain, smoking.

Paths through the fields, which lead in to the political.

Once we came to a bridge you could only cross one at a time. It swayed. A few people did not try at all, and stayed behind.

One was looking for a stone to throw into the water, but did not find a stone.

After a pause, into which silence had entered, it remained silent.

Two ravens sitting in a cage. A sign says that the two ravens were born in the cage.

In the dream he finally reached the station. But by then the station was already gone.

We don't have a whole lot in our hand, the trainer says, but we'll follow through with what we do.

From somewhere the sound of voices. All of a sudden they stopped, and one heard a bus driving away.

Crumbling letters on a wall. They are Russian letters.

Wooden structures marking the way, the Office of Public Roads says.

He constantly looked at the clock, but the time, which usually went so quickly, was now moving in the tiniest of increments.

A quick goodbye when one is the last.

Why one forgets the furnishings of a hotel room so quickly.

Were you on holiday? No, in the garden.

In the past, when one turned on the radio, one would sit down and listen.

We are supposed to have said that?

In the evenings rabbits appeared.

The first one can, but does not have to. The second one has to, but cannot.

What one fears when the call doesn't come.

Put your cars away, or we'll set them on fire.

One counts to sixty. Then one has a whole minute.

Not all that many people came, somewhere else there is more is going on.

Soon Greenland will be free.

What we will miss when no one lies any more.

An empty plate out on the meadow. The crows.

One's supposed to have an opinion. But you don't. If someone comes along asking, you'll have to come up with something suitable.

The painter doesn't know what the forester knows. He paints the trees.

Protest is desired. Resistance is requested.

For a long-distance call one dialled zero. An operator answered. One gave one's own number and asked to be connected with the desired number. Then one hung up and waited. After some time, the phone rang. It was the operator. She either said: The person you have dialled does not answer. Or: The person you have dialled is unavailable. If the connection was made, she said: Your connection. And connected you.

Tomatoes are available all year.

A man is standing in the doorway to the courtyard, peeing.

After the rain, the birds start to sing again.

*The filling-station attendant says, If Monday is a holiday too, the price of fuel stays up.*

People are standing in front of the church. After some time, they go inside.

Often, when Father came back from the telephone, he had a serious face.

Does one know anyone who still beats their carpet?

The wall closet was full of suitcases. That is not where you looked for him.

Flipping through the calendar asking oneself how much longer.

One's been invited for tonight. What could one say in order to cancel.

It had to be something important, to make a long-distance call.

A summer dress with large flowers. Because it is an old black-and-white photograph, you can't say any thing about the colours.

In the past, we had a carpet beater in the courtyard.

The chair one wants to sit in is on the other side of the table.

Thirty soldiers. Looking more closely, thirty officers.

Horse-drawn carriages, gasoline carriages.

In the middle, it occurs to one how challenging it was to learn how to read and write.

There aren't many people in the restaurant. They are wearing hats, and they aren't eating either.

Outside it appears to be quiet. In any event, one doesn't hear any thing inside.

There are countries where it is now dark.

One gets hungry, multiple times a day, and every day one has enough to eat.

There were a few who were really nice.

One managed to find a stone, but now there isn't any water.

The sun was shining, we stood in the doorway watching a dogfight.

The one has made a threat. Now we have to wait to see what the other will do.

The heavy man has lost weight. But he's heavy all the same.

Your skin is ageing. Do you know why?

At night the deer are in the garden. The garden has a fence.

If you're feeling happy, be careful.

We made a mistake somewhere, otherwise the gutter would not be dripping.

Hurry up. We won't be here much longer.

One meets others and the first thing one hears is how
good one looks.

The old photographer talks about how he set up ladders,
built scaffolding, got rid of trees.

The person you have called is not available.

A jay lands in the cherry tree. A second jay lands in
the cherry tree.

What is going through a person's head when they've set
a car on fire?

Eating a ham sandwich. The ham is too salty.

You don't understand all that much any more, a person
said, but you get by.

You should have seen your face.

The airfield, the airdrome, the airport.

A gust of wind, a shutter flies open, the room grows light.

Didn't we want to emigrate once?

He was surprised. Or, in any event, he acted as if he were.

Demonstrators trampling the farmer's field, peaceful
demonstrators.

Where the map turned green, that's where the North
German Plain began.

In the mornings a man goes to the train station to drink
a beer.

Ah, the North German Plain.

The small tractor won't start. One is at a loss, but in any
event opens the hood and has a look.

One has a seat and counts to sixty again. That can take
a whole hour.

When he awoke, he saw a round, yellow hole glowing
in the black sky.

*Tuesday. The man has come for the tractor. He already
had a new battery with him.*

The hedgehog doesn't show up during the day.

Two men speaking with each other. They are wearing head-
phones and are one hour by flight away from each other.

Cherry pancakes at noon.

Storms have been announced. Clear the garden table.

In the past the mice would leave the house in summer.

Hydrangeas, bluer than ever.

Are you allowed to buy oats and feed them to the birds?

What else is one supposed to see, a few photos are enough.

Those who plant rice do not paint grain fields.

Why does one have to start work so early?

If you go to the kiosk early enough, all the newspapers
are still there.

One shower after the other. Here and there the sun.
Put another way, the sun is always shining, here and there
a shower.

You meet outdoors and sit under a walnut tree. You
drink Portuguese white wine. Two men talk to each other.
The protocol records that one of the two yells a number
of times.

Once we ran into each other on the street again. It was
already dark, and the lights were on in the pub on the
other side of the street.

Waking during the night, then getting up to check one's
daily appointment calendar.

One bowl for the raspberries. One bowl for the gooseberries.

One asks oneself why there is a helicopter circling over
the house at such an early hour.

Voices in a distant garden. Many voices, female voices,
mixed, quick, excited. Then, as if cut, everything is quiet.

Someone comes up the stairs and then goes back down.

Officially you don't know a thing, but in the evenings

when someone stops by for a visit you don't talk about anything else.

Every day, but only a little.

There are rivers that peter out along the way.

You can buy rolls at the butcher's. You cannot buy meat at the baker's.

In the dream a rival of yours sits down at the table, a former rival who, whenever you'd run into him, ruined the day with his offensive behaviour and icy manners. Now he is quite friendly, even addresses you informally. You hope that he'll disappear again immediately, but he only disappears once the dream breaks off.

Two small buckets. One for the cherries, one for the red currants.

There are people who find a parking spot right away.

Someone calls and asks if you have any old materials. Well, in the shed there are a few beams from the half-timbered house, a small box with nails and screws, a piece of gutter, some tar paper, a few bricks too . . . The caller, however, was asking about documentary material, in particular, sketches, concepts, scores, texts, photographs, newspaper articles, posters.

Whenever we had to clean, this and that got lost.

One knows about those in hiding, but cannot find them.

The kitchen table is older than the man leaning his arms upon it.

Someone wants to begin here. Had he stopped somewhere?

An island of which one has heard that it slowly is becoming too small.

It only looks like everything in the garden repeats. It only looks like that at times.

Sometimes small amounts are enough.

He says he is too old for new furniture.

The number of the dead are asked to be included.

There are living beings in the building who one never sees.

It's not war, but there are enemies in the country.

Once Father said, Do not stand by the window.

Low-lying clouds, almost at eye level.

There are still a few farmers in town. They have city addresses.

He does not want to say who his friends are.

Three weeks ago the old photographer was still alive. He came up to the table where everyone knew him, everyone but one, to whom he introduced himself with the words, I'm your son's teacher.

Those who could afford it had the exposed sides of their half-timbered houses covered in slate.

Don't you believe that you have a guardian angel?

The woodpecker must wait. First the jay.

Watching a child smash his soft-boiled egg.

He walks across the field. Breathes deep. Stretches out his arms and moves them in circles, at first slowly, then quicker and quicker.

The doctor gave a warning. The moderator wanted to know. The architect made a suggestion. The mayor did not answer.

*On Wednesday the man had to come for the tractor once again. This time he brought a new fan belt.*

Who are you thinking about when you say that certain names have been forgotten?

In the waiting room there are magazines that one would never read otherwise.

One knows why one is happy.

The motorway is so quiet this morning. What's going on?

Young people are going to stop by; he pulls his oldest suit out of the closet.

There isn't any wind either, it's just that the parasol has fallen over.

The newspaper is delivered at five in the morning. If you get up, you immediately have something to read.

Coffee or tea?

Fuel is expensive today, the station attendant says, but if it gets even more expensive tomorrow, today will have been cheap.

Do you still write everything by hand?

Fuel up in the evening. Sleep at night. Drive on the next day.

Do we feel something we usually don't?

We reached the coast the same day. Immense cloud landscapes, and we sat down.

One can see how far one can see.

The reason for repetition.

A watch like an old hand-wound watch.

Well, here you all are again. Indeed. Here we are again.

A tea set with a few defects. We bring old newspapers with us.

Do you all care for the construction sites in the village?

The post has already arrived too, a book with empty pages.

The old female painter, in between stacks of paintings. She says, I have decided not to paint any more.

The cracks in the wall of the house have not grown,
and there do not appear to be any new cracks.

Swans at flight. Before one sees them, the raucous calls,
the rushing of their wings.

A few of the old people here were once refugee children.
They talk about how they were informed that they had
been resettled.

Auntie says her nephew doesn't know that he is the son of
the sister who was raped.

Are you in the file as well?

One knows that being a painter of marine scenes doesn't
mean one's got to be in the marines.

When he did not need any contacts, then, because he
had them.

Plum pancakes at noon.

The expanses of sky blue, meadow green and sea grey.

Having grown too tall the hollyhocks fold over.

We never signed a thing.

The owners died in the West. They never saw the hotel in
the East again. There is still some tableware in the building.

The room is dark, one sits outside.

The woman next door thinks for a long time before any recent news comes to mind.

What is one looking for in old, empty coat pockets?

That the doctor calls in the afternoon and wants to know how one is doing.

Do we see everything?

If you count all the newspapers you throw out every day, you know how many days have passed.

The intercity bus has a bicycle rack for bicycles.

The woman comes to a family reunion, more than three hundred people. Old landed gentry, at one time established in the area.

We did not see Father again.

Nuns fluttering across the sands.

If you move closer to the painting, you can see that the landscape is made up of pieces of different landscapes.

Yet another article that only names the same three, four names.

You walked through the park and at the end the fields began, and stretched all the way to the horizon.

He stood next to the sunflower and saw that it was a whole head taller.

Do we know everything?

The horse came back with the empty wagon.

Polish was being spoken, but one was not in Poland.

One cannot really say who the first were any longer.

A person moves back into the countryside, to an isolated village where hardly anyone lives any more and to which no one comes. They make sure that every one knows.

The blackberries. Green, then red, now black.

Before the travellers arrive, their personal information has already been received.

Buildings that recall buildings.

There are ways of living together that do not go peacefully.

A Bodden landscape, with a stormy atmosphere.

Children. Few witness the end of the century.

The cyclist rings his bell because you didn't hear him approach.

On the way it begins to rain. Did you close the windows?

Was it ever the case that you could have said, Now I've answered every letter?

Woken up by the sound of furniture being moved.

In one of the abandoned houses a light still burned.

The names have been changed, but one knows who the people are.

One only took what was theirs.

As children we really didn't have any idea.

Fingerprints. Certification.

The summer uniform suited the boy. He smiled as he introduced himself and said, I can become rather unpleasant.

*It was Thursday, and many trains were not running.*

The way back was long, but the horse knew the way.

The blue-onion patterned tableware. The record collection. The stamp album. The hat case. The dog whip. The pin cushion. The dress uniform.

We had to give up our schoolbooks. Some days later they were returned. Missing certain pages, some of the passages blacked out.

All of a sudden he was overcome by rage and began to sweep dishes off the table.

Sometimes it's enough to stand at the window. If not, one only has to tap the pane once to scare off the magpies.

Did you overlook the gun cabinet? No, but there weren't any guns there.

Elderberry blossoms. Coltsfoot leaves.

The briefcase was under his head.

Horex. Zündapp.

The circus wagon is coming into the village. Get the
laundry inside.

Once he got home and was sitting in the kitchen, he asked,
What year is it anyway?

A green-looking Mercedes is being pushed into the shop.
It was out in the meadow for eighteen years.

Apple pancakes at noon.

We marched to the edge of town and gathered herbs
for the wounded.

He says, If you say everything, there's nothing left to say.

He reached for the glass, which was already empty,
a number of times.

Sometimes people from the past showed back up.

Later on.

So we did know everything?

According to the headlines summer is coming back. Had
it gone already?

Under different names.

You see a man walking, but he does not seem to move.

Eagle. Wanderer.

Older listeners still know.

The man was Dutch. But then it turned out he wasn't.

He sat in front of his shadow and was surprised that it was larger than his body.

So, tell me, how much longer do you intend to drive your old off-road vehicle?

Could a bat really hinder the construction of a bridge?

A postcard of winter, in Sweden, in the last century.

Why did you buy a kilo of beans but then immediately throw them away?

One sees a few islands are on fire.

When you simply let people go, they soon turn up again.

Up until the end the suitcases were in the wall closet. Large old suitcases. He could not separate himself from them. You never know, he said.

Those who have to go out at night have to cross the courtyard.

To get to the plums we simply sawed off the branches which were towering over the roof.

Why do people who don't smoke get lung cancer?

He was lying on the banks of the river, dreaming of lying on the banks of the river.

After school holidays, the class essay. My most wonderful holiday experience.

Who knows who said eat fish and you will stay healthy?

Once it had come into the village, the mayor was waiting with a pot of coffee on a tray.

When it began to rain, the pieces of furniture that had been removed from the houses were in the rain.

Can't we finally stop?

Mother wanted to, Father did not.

One could hear the glasses rattling in the cupboard. Nothing more.

Those who did not want to be noticed, were not noticed.

Later, later on.

You could not take a lot, and you did not immediately know what you should take with you.

Perhaps one does not want to find any thing at all where one seeks.

In the heat the smell of tar.

Once you've read today's paper, you know more than
you did yesterday.

How often it is, he said, that I don't have an answer,
but have to answer anyway.

When we got to the place, we saw how tall the grass
had grown.

How long ago was that?

Ageing he encounters ghosts with ever more frequency.

And that wasn't all, not by a long shot.

With a bicycle you got away more quickly.

The border: that was the path through the fields, the course
of the stream, the edge of the woods.

He did not find any traces, and the people that he asked
were young.

A brief lag, then the off-road vehicle gave a yelp.

Once, our friend the landscape painter went to go paint
with a permit.

*Chausseen Chausseen* by Huchel.

No one had to order us, we knew what it had to do with.

It was a windmill that one could rotate, and often
the miller rotated it westwards.

Once a swan came swimming across the pond. It was not a swan, but a fake swan, beneath which appeared the head of a swimmer.

In the meantime does anyone know what happened to the forester who disappeared?

The men who ordered a 'brown' received brown schnapps.

We were Prussians too, the person from the Rhineland said.

A few people knew that an antenna had been installed inside the windmill.

Returning home and hearing the pump, we knew that the cellar was underwater.

You don't have to go away for memory.

A radio on the table.

Should one get up and go look why a door slammed shut somewhere in the house?

A person who collaborated accuses others of collaboration.

One refuses to accept any comparison.

In the past, the registered mail carrier would come.

He washed his hands beforehand too.

Damson plums are a bit smaller than regular plums.

The filling-station attendant says, One way or the other, by eleven the weather will have made up its mind.

*Fridays the women would come to pick us up. Because of the pay packet. Some men would blow half of their week's wages at the pub already.*

Greenland is planting potatoes, tomatoes.

The long, warm summer days before the war.

A stretch of Reichsautobahn. It was almost empty.

It happens that, after ten years, one uses the same sentence once again.

Fieseler Storch.

The boy parted his hair on the right.

He knew a lot of nouns. Not a lot of things.

The long, warm summer days after the war.

Get to work, it will set you free.

Damson-plum pancakes at noon.

Sometimes Father would remain seated and demonstrate how to blow smoke rings into the air.

A chair on its side, and a few steps further the view out the open window onto the wall of the house opposite.

The rain is coming in to the room. One goes and shuts the window.

The miller was picked up.

Land. Lake. Figures.

In the room there are pictures. In the room there are black figures, white structures, the *Hohe Ufer* journal, the water-edged woods, West Beach on Darß, weather fronts.

To make visible what there is to see.

A man crosses the street, carrying a board.

One observes people who do not know that they are being observed.

He says, I have opinions that I can only share with myself.

Cucumbers are growing in the garden. One goes in to the garden to get a cucumber.

He left the house with wet shoes.

Can you hear the excavator?

And they did not take just anyone.

Does one know anyone who comes up with puzzles, invents jokes?

One says, I've always been lucky. I was either overlooked, forgotten or the train was delayed.

In the radio that's on the table you can hear the sea.

Hard pears. Wasps burrow in and hollow them out.

The arch-enemy, who was that?

He says, In the past, we all knew one another.

In these woods the women hid themselves with their children.

It's becoming evening, and the ice cubes clink in the glass.

Navy-blue suits. Light-grey vehicles.

Two chairs on the road, a man walking back and forth between them.

The squirrel has come.

He gets up and says, I don't know what I want.

Ivy growing in to the house, and if you don't do any thing, it will continue to grow.

After waking one knows that one has to get up.

Father, while eating mushrooms, talked about a family he knew that died after eating mushrooms.

In the background, between the trees, there is a person raising their right arm.

Later he began to accept invitations again and to mix with others.

Because of the air one can see that, at the end of the cratered landscape, the trees along the water-side path are casting shadows on the river.

The bus driver says, If there are any problems, the bus just stops.

By noon the fog was gone, and we were back in the sun.

You cannot see the man's head. He is behind the board that the man is carrying across the street.

He threw balls of paper into the corner of the room for so long that the corner became full of balls of paper.

He did not do so happily, but what other choice did he have.

Go away, moth, back into the night.

Every sentence, he says, stands within an environment of other sentences that the author did not write.

With her male-sounding name she often received mail addressed to a man.

Up there the heron is flying. When we see the heron, we say, Up there the heron is flying.

Good morning, postman. Good morning, roofer. Good morning, milkman.

A long story, and he did not know any longer how it had begun either.

A fence so that nothing gets away.

In the morning, the cushions were still on the floor.

He mowed the first half before it rained, the other after it rained.

One would go for a walk with a walking stick.

A banister you can pull yourself up with.

The lamp is hanging so low that you cannot see the faces.

Difficulty swallowing, and one has to think of the deceased, how it started that way.

The dream: a family reunion, a family which for the most part has died out.

One wonders whether the old record player still works. One wants to play the old records.

*Saturday, the first day of September, the first page in Hart-laub's war diaries.*

The green apples stay green.

The ground was like ash in the tobacco fields where women, together with their small children, would pick tobacco leaves.

One has quotes that keep the story alive.

Once, the off-road vehicle stood on the banks of the Oder. After some time, it turned around.

In the evening, on the phone, a friend said she would be getting on her bicycle to do the shopping for the evening.

Before you go out, you get dressed.

Must we always be tolerant?

He knew the precise dates. But when he was asked what he could remember he said, Nothing.

Tobacco front. Mon plaisir. Coastal defence. Meadows. Night watches. The place. Farmers and soldiers.

He cannot drink white wine. So he drinks red.

When the sun disappears behind a cloud, it immediately turns cold.

Old rooms. Crevices between the floorboards, pine needles, hairpins, pins, dust.

Pushed to eat something, he ate nothing.

The taxi driver keeps a pack of Gitanes in the glove box. I have for thirty years, he says, but now, when I'm waiting on a fare, I'm not even allowed to smoke in my own car.

Old train station, late-night transport.

Is there a broom here?

One walks into an empty pub and realizes it isn't empty.

If we figure out the beginning, can we repeat it?

Nothing stood out to the neighbours. They have only positive things to say.

Tomato pancakes at noon.

Whatever you leave out is not there.

Someone calls and immediately hangs back up.

A lot of people confirmed. A lot of people did not show up.

One turns towards the exit. That is where one will discuss where to meet shortly thereafter.

Those are young people, and they get a start by copying every thing.

It's better to screw them in, he said, you can unscrew them later.

We couldn't see any thing, he said, but we returned fire.

If you are only familiar with three kinds of mushrooms, you do not collect four.

One was looking for two men and uncovered a network.

The postcards were postcards.

Our people were not there. If our people had been there, things would have been different.

One sees that there are green apples that turn yellow.

Do you like cats? Do you like mice?

The missing forester was under suspicion. That is why
he disappeared.

You do not abandon your vehicle as long as it still drives.

Do we have everything? Will we make it through the
weekend?

He takes photographs of the shadows he casts. But in the
photographs you not only see his shadow, but the objects
beneath his shadow: the grass, the path, the street, the floor,
the wall, the stairs, the water.

Did we make a mistake? And if we did, will it lead to a crisis?

Before you forget everything, please make a list.

A bird falling from the sky. And as it falls, begins to fly.

The way it is when you dig up horseradish, peel and grate
the roots, the way its smell goes to your head.

The plains of September light. The angles at the edge of
the woods. The debris of nuts.

Unfamiliar mushrooms. We compare them to mushrooms
with which we are familiar.

If he had possessed the courage he was reputed to have,
he would have stopped.

A bag, a pouch, a sack.

In the middle of a telephone conversation he suddenly said:
A deer is springing across the meadow. The caller asked,
What do you mean? He said, he meant what he could see
through the window, the meadow, the garden, the bushes,
the trees, a deer, a rarity during the day, suddenly appearing
between the bushes and springing across the meadow.

One memory gap after another, when one attempts to call
back to mind the moments of the past day. So we say that it
is pure chance that we suddenly found the keys, under the
chair, where the trousers are hanging, out of whose pockets
they must have fallen.

The off-road vehicle rolls in to the barn, a radio broadcast
breaks off.

He comes from the Rhenish Slate Mountains, the roofer
says, but the slate he is working with comes from Spain.

The neighbour is in hospital. Her daughter crossed the
courtyard to say so. Since Thursday. That is, the day before
yesterday. No, sorry, since last Thursday.

The mail carrier brings ever more letters that one can
see one does not even have to open.

At night sometimes he would turn on the radio. Seldom
during the day.

He looked at his watch, and to do so pushed back his sleeve.

One time you win, one time you lose (Stan Kenton).

The addresses are still lying there, with all the old postal codes.

If something cracks underfoot, it means you're walking over hazelnuts.

Do have any memories about the street where you live?

The sun has risen. You don't see any sun.

When were postal codes even introduced? When the Nazis were in power. But they're still around. Sure, but you can't put it that way.

He painted the garden fence until there was no paint left in the bucket.

Could the wasp be threatening the sleeping man?

He showed the way, without realizing that someone would imitate it.

He said, If I think about it a while, it begins to scare me.

The phone has been dead for two days already.

The cardinal says what one cannot.

The cheese is three days old. It can get even older.

Take care of your children, please, or they'll steal the apples off our tree.

*On Sundays, the filling-station attendant says, some people come just to get the Sunday paper.*

One tells the cardinal he cannot say what he just said.

On the third day, out of the blue the telephone rings.

Four men sitting at a table. In the middle there is a woman. She is asking questions. The men answer.

Both neighbours agree. The one did not have to think about it long at all, the other hesitated for quite some time.

From far away, the sound of a brass band. It seems to get closer, but it does not get any closer.

When nothing occurs to you, three minutes are a long time.

Once we stood on a wooden bridge and looked down onto the bright lines of the empty Reichsautobahn. It was still under construction and, for the time being, no one was working.

One sees a young mother with her two boys, both with their backs to the photographer, standing in the photographer's shadow on the street.

The road corresponds to the route. But one does not recognize it. The once empty land around it has been developed, and the people who once walked there are gone.

The way to school in the mornings lasted ten minutes. Dawdling home took him fortyfive.

Shortly after the Catholics had joined the Protestants in class, the war broke out.

Half a roll, a piece of blackbread, in-between a slice of Emmentaler cheese.

Dawdle, one of the many words he heard for the first time from his mother.

You got what you needed, and what you did not get did not exist.

If we stand in the garden we can see the disparity.

Does the weather ask what it should be like?

Once she came back home with an apron full of corncobs.

The beam is wobbly, the one says. It always has been, says the other.

The old stove, it's still cold.

Anyone who carries a letter is a letter carrier. (Müntefering.)

Strangers who greet each other on the roads are on motorcycles.

Between the ones in uniform is a person playing the accordion.

In July, she said, there were so many blueberries we would go into the woods with buckets.

One got the names out of the telephone book.

Summer during the day, autumn at night.

What we are missing is an umbrella stand.

As he grew taller, he could look into the wall mirror, and whenever he walked by, he'd cast a glance.

We have, he says, a neighbour who writes us a letter every autumn. We know what he's going to write. It has to do with the hedge, the height of the hedge, two or three centimetres.

If you belonged, you received blueberries to eat.

They caught the burglar as he was breaking into a house, but since he has a fixed address, he is allowed to go back home.

There is a package in front of the door. Were you expecting a package?

He couldn't dance, but the way he moved looked like dancing.

Not like that, the old workman would say, like this.

Going to look at the trees in the afternoon.

In the empty coffee cup a grape. One wonders how it got there.

Who are these people one dreams about but doesn't know?

One can hear something buzzing about the room.

One sees a man write his name on a photograph in which he himself appears.

He's got ideas.

Across the way the window is open, and one can hear someone whistling.

One still doesn't know how to deal with it.

Someone has sold their property and says, I didn't want to sell it at all.

The lane disappears into the fog from which the tractor appears.

One can hear a mechanical saw refusing to start.

Some say, When it gets cold, we're going to fly south.

Silent storms.

He turned the radio on. Listened to the news. Turned the radio off.

It doesn't matter, he says, if you don't know whether all the languages spoken are also understood.

In the past, when we still had colonies, there were stores where we bought colonial goods.

The air route was short, then one had to wait.

One entered a room where pieces of clothing were strewn across the floor.

*On Monday you know what's behind you. You do not know what's ahead.*

What it's like when you close the front door and get in to the waiting taxi.

If we don't have to travel, why do we want to?

The reality of a prospect.

Figures step out of a poem and sit down on the terrace wall.

Tentative titles for emerging images.

Did you personally know any Surrealists?

After a number of long answers, he needed to pause for breath.

The mountain promises a view. In order for the mountain to deliver on its promise, one has to climb it.

Did others think what he thought?

He kept two diaries. One in the morning, the other in the evening. In the morning he wrote what he intended to do with the day. In the evening what had come of his plans.

High above the sea there's an old church which was built for sailors in trouble.

In the midday heat the white wall was so white you could not look at it.

A woman, crying loudly, crosses the street.

The sky grew darker and darker, until it was completely black.

You see tiny, unfamiliar animals.

The strange sunshine; she asks for darker lenses.
The optician says, There aren't any.

Half-horse, half-donkey.

If you go into the sea to walk, you don't get far.

In the morning green, in the evening yellow lemons.

Going through the hallway of a hotel where you are not
a guest.

The crying woman is in the supermarket. She is taken
by the hand and led outside.

The mobile rings. They ask where we are.

In the dream he takes off his coat and gets spooked, for
the jacket he was wearing underneath his coat is missing.

The mule between the taxi drivers.

The problem will remain if no one gets up to clean the dishes.

During the night there was heavy wind and there was
nothing to do but straighten the terrace in the morning.

The man shaves every morning. Sometimes he asks himself,
Why do I shave every morning?

Looking out through the door of the church, in the interior
courtyard, one can see a palm tree.

Hearing someone say that half the time is gone.

We lost sight of one another, the narrator says of his figures.

A rose for the mausoleum of the painter from Berlin.

The old hotel has closed. The heirs were too young.

Not knowing the answer but saying something anyway
can lead to disaster.

Flat roofs with deck chairs.

How one walks down the hill, along the beach, up the hill.

The reptile coming closer is a small salamander.

Do you really want to know all that's going on at home?

One's got to assume that what's caused the road behind
the bend to be closed is a landslide.

To awake and to try and dream the dream that's been
ripped away again. You never get back.

One can see that a few decades have changed things more
than a few centuries.

Why you're happy when, after a year, they recognize you
at the *trattoria*.

Completely alone, the crescent moon above the sea.

Appliances are being recharged at night.

Hotel corridor with a view onto the sea. Dialogues between guests who see each other here year after year and who by now are old. They seem to say the same thing over and over, when they see one another, when they leave, like being stuck in an absurdist piece of theatre.

He says, When I don't want to think about anything heavy, I lay down in the sun.

The handwriting is thin. The wind cold. The view clear.

He hears the locals speaking about snow. Although it never snows. But there's a wind from the north and it's autumn, and the temperature is dropping.

Someone asks about the way. When you don't know, you offer a helpless little smile. When you do, you immediately take up the role of the expert, affably informative, tolerantly smiley.

One says, The moon has made a yard. If one isn't understood immediately, one says, A yard has been made by the moon.

The paper arrives a day later now. Because it's autumn, they said at the kiosk.

Sun-warm tomatoes, once upon a time.

Everyone rushed. Now they are all standing around waiting.

You sit in a plane and watch it makes its way across a map.

*It was a Tuesday when the first maple leaves fell.*

A letter was returned due to the lack of a house number. They have lived on the same street for decades and there are only a few houses.

As we were away, we missed a funeral. The one who died had even wished us a pleasant journey.

A notebook of drawings has disappeared. In the evening it's back.

She says, Because I'm by myself, when I leave my apartment I leave a light on.

He changed benches in order not to see the rat that was under the bench facing him.

One sees a woman carrying two bags full of leaves into the woods.

One hears that the cranes are still in Mecklenburg.

The woods, if not for long, are yellow.

Notes found again which had been written for a later time that is long past.

The sealed letterbox, the discontinued post office.

Once he had begun to experience habit as an adventure.

Someone reminds him of a high-rise where he once lived. He doesn't know any longer on which floor exactly.

The shortest night is the one when you sleep all the way through.

Forced by the day to stay inside all day.

An orchard in November.

Going to the bottle bin, you have to differentiate between the green, white and brown bottles.

Upon hearing his voice, he left the room.

What's with those relatives one doesn't know anything about.

One had gone to hear music, but that wasn't music.

Whenever something fell to the ground, he'd immediately bend down.

There are a few left. Who should we ask?

He hears people saying sentences which are identical to the ones he is writing.

One keeps all of the keys together and has to go through each of them before being able to unlock the old door.

There aren't too many houses where a door has not been opened in a long time.

Does everyone agree with the name they've been given?

Those who go to work early are now driving in the dark.

Designs for a space that does not yet exist.

In the window one sees the same lamp two times.

One doesn't have anything to do and goes to bed early.

In a photograph a woman with an armful of bread. Walking through the desert.

In the desert there are refugees who are so quiet that they have been forgotten.

How the theme of the day forms.

One doesn't say anything about it because one doesn't know.

In the past every man had a briefcase, and it clicked when shut.

You cannot sit outside any more. Why is the garden furniture still outside?

He can write numbers, he cannot add.

Mild days of rain, cold days of sun.

A few officers belonged to their circle of acquaintances. Some had wives. One could see that they were the wives of officers.

It's dripping here, but from where?

There are nails, but no hammer.

A forest owner says, I have a forest full of wood.

He had hoped it was an accident. It wasn't an accident.

There's no going forward. And everything behind us is blocked.

If the doorbell rings in the early morning, it's the two brick-layers. The one is from Slovenia, the other from Masuria.

Sitting in the room one sees two horses, two women, a church tower, a spruce forest, a collapsed roof.

The way one sees an area that no longer exists.

Sometimes he tries to re-experience past experience. Sometimes he is successful.

First he pulled on his winter coat, then he put on his hat.

How could one tell that they were officers?

The last tram would depart at one in the morning. Other-wise one had to wait until four o'clock for the first tram.

Memory arrives once it knows that it will be picked up by a few words.

The egg cup has no egg. The salt shaker has no salt. The schnapps glass is empty. If you plan to do something about it, you can't stay in your chair.

A woman, scrubbing the floor on her hands and knees.

Often, in winter, Father would sit in front of the tiled stove with his back. The stove was almost as big as he was, and Father was a big man.

A man walking across the fields, coming from the water-works. He is looking for the old water line. He is using a dowsing rod.

Daisies in December.

Haven't heard the owl in a long time. Tonight it's sitting in front of the kitchen window.

The neighbour has set a trap for the marten. It has caught the hedgehog, the cat, the squirrel.

The electrician explains how he installs Christmas lights.

A small goat comes in to the kitchen.

*Wednesday morning it never gets light. One puts on a white shirt.*

The bricklayers are working on two sites. They go back and forth. Or one is here, and the other there.

People come to get their fuel, the filling-station attendant says, but they don't need me to do that.

A bird flies by. You don't have much time to see it.

If one hasn't smoked in decades, why does the skin get older anyway?

Iced-over windscreens. Scraping noises early.

He says, There are connections one doesn't see. Should one just believe it?

Time has passed, and one asks about certain names. Then it has to do with whether a lot of time or little time has passed.

What is the off-road vehicle doing? It's busy. Moving chairs, firewood, bags of leaves.

Once, in the moonlight, one saw the frost gleaming on the fields.

Once, he noticed that he had put on his sweater backwards.

She caught a cold while she was on the phone.

In the afternoon getting ready for evening.

There are people who die during Christmas.

The little girl explains why one sees the same lamp in the window two times.

Behind the window is a man. In front of the window a cat.

Which novels should one read now?

The garden light goes on; the motion detector registered some kind of movement. One goes to the window and looks outside.

In every street more cars than there are garages.

During the day you don't see the tiny bulbs that light up in the dark in the bushes and trees.

The news of accidents during Christmas.

During the twelve days of Christmas women do not
do the laundry.

The pencil waits for the hand to move it. The hand waits
for something to make it move the pencil.

He stepped out the door in order to take a walk around
the courtyard. But when he saw snowflakes, he paused.

Where the stairs make a bend, there is a painting on the
wall. In it a street making a bend in the same direction.

He stood up, went into another room and sat down.

Did you find where it was leaking?

On the chair next to the bed: a glass and a bottle of water.

The vase filled with water burst with the frost. One clears
the pieces of glass but leaves the frozen water behind.

If he's been forgotten, then he's the one responsible.

One sees how in Karelia people say, That is not discussed.

Can one call it writing if one types?

Finding support with one's hands when a ladder slips
away under one's feet.

At midnight the explosions would start. Tracers, shrapnel,
rockets, flak. Smoke would drift through the streets.

You had to shut your windows.

One reads that someone is selling journals in which he'd written intimate details.

He says he doesn't write any stories, for then he would have to come to an end. On the contrary, he writes in order to come to a beginning.

Lying down one thinks differently than standing up.

Does one already need another new year?

When you have to scream in your dream, you immediately wake up.

Empty gardens in January.

*Thursday scrambled eggs, potato salad, Spreewald pickles.*

Mother never went to the dentist.

Every series eventually ends.

The puddle he jumped over was iced.

Sometimes, when coming out of the cellar, he'd bring rotten apples.

He'd got used to it, he said, putting his sweater on the wrong way.

You don't remember? Well, in any event, that's the way it was.

In the past, there was an ashtray on every table.

In town there was a novelist one seldom saw. When
you asked about him, people would say he was busy
interviewing Sisyphus.

One gets further when one goes to sit at a different table.

Considering doing something which makes movement,
space, an outline.

Once one got the garden gate open, one could go into
the garden.

Someone whose call you'd been waiting for called. Says
that he'll come. Now you are waiting for him to come.

The saleswoman at the door has travelled from the Elbe.
She has potatoes from Lüneberg Heath, apples from
Altes Land, outside of Hamburg.

When there's frost, the filling-station attendant says,
you  can still have your car washed, but not when there's
heavy frost.

To slowly eat an apple, an apple that's been cut into four.

Does the village really need a second store? The village says
yes, the store says no.

Didn't understand a thing, but fascinating.

One watches an East German playing a northern Italian.

The store where you wanted to buy something at nine
only opens at eleven.

Every series begins with something that, at the beginning,
is something new.

The painting you want to see isn't there.

I never said, he says, Because I didn't know, I am now
saying the right or the wrong thing.

You could open the window, but once it was open it
was loud and cold.

When school finally began again, after the war, the teachers
said, Good morning.

A sausage stand. A chips stand. A potato-pancake stand.

A neighbour asked us to not feed his cat.

Nails are being hammered into the wall. To hang pictures.

If you have the time for it, you can see how the twilight
comes. One doesn't have a lot of time for that.

Suddenly you are standing in front of a stream. Those who
know the sentence know that it has to do with a French
limousine that is stopped in front of a stream.

When the stew was half done, the pot was placed into
a box and the box into the bed. That was what was
known as a haybox.

In the room in the hall a candle is burning.

Appointments, appointments, all excuses.

The saleswoman from the Elbe, one watches her drive
off in a van with a registration number from the region
of the Ruhr.

The bag is full. One ties it shut.

The description could not be any more precise. Where
was the problem?

Some of the women turned towards the viewer.

The gallery was empty. In order to see the exhibition,
you walked up to the window and looked onto the street.

The second orchestra was directed by Karlheinz
Stockhausen.

# Journal Three

The concert took place in a hall that had not been conceived
of for concerts.

One could hear them, the trains off behind the woods.

The linden tree, two hundred years old, was under
monumental protection. Ever since fungus spread through
its branches, it has not been under protection.

Sometimes the off-road vehicle was parked in the shade
of the linden tree.

Those who don't care to smoke can leave the room.

Another photo, at that time in uniform.

The tobacconist has moved to a store that is smaller
and cheaper.

Why weren't the tracks bombed?

Was someone looking for the photo or was it found
by accident?

The general's daughter married a gardener.

From outside you can see where the key is hanging.

The electric meter has begun to hum, and immediately one
calls the electrician. He knocks on the side a few times,
and the humming stops.

So did the Russians pay the rent and the electricity?

Fur hats, fur collars, fur boots.

In the dream two crutches helped him walk along the foot-
wide path. The crutches reached down to the street, an
almost 30-metre drop.

Somewhere close by there's some kind of engine room
with machines that run non-stop.

The guard who waved to us had the face of a child.

Fried potatoes for breakfast already.

Go bring your father to the table.

We just had wooden guns, and when we shot them,
we imitated the sounds guns make.

The building is familiar. The old car park. The curve the
same. But the entrance has been changed.

Until recently, the name was common. Now you no longer encounter the name.

Winter sun. Deep in the sky the whole day. The whole day as if blinded.

Two men, one woman, the film.

Those who weren't there do not understand why it turned out that way.

Two were already there, then the third arrived.

In the parents' front yard, a flagpole.

Once the young pastor had taken off his cassock, he was wearing an officer's uniform.

Was he under suspicion?

At times his wife earned their income.

In some of the yards the inhabitants had constructed bunkers. Later, they stored potatoes in them. Or apples. The two did not tolerate each other; which is to say, the apples did not tolerate the potatoes, and immediately began to rot.

The small shovel belonged to a Pioneer.

Not a lot of older female teachers. All of them were unmarried, younger women.

The left hand protects the flame, the right holds the lighter.

There were glasses on the table. But he drank from the bottle.

When the lieutenant came into the kitchen, he brought a pail of herring and an arm full of onions.

Sometimes there would be a lorry in the courtyard. When he saw that it was full of wood, he'd go into the cellar.

When there was frost, he'd leave the house without taking a shower.

They found Uncle up in the storage room. He'd immediately gone up to the storage room.

The accordion's sigh.

It's noon; one wants to go to sleep.

In the past, the post was already there in the morning.

A light is on in both the upper-storey windows. If you only see one, you're either in front of the house or behind it.

The bread bag had belonged to a telephone operator.

The film begins with a corpse, lying in the woods, for days already, already before the film began.

There are coats in the wardrobe, more coats than people in the house.

A narrator appears. One recognizes him from an earlier
book. He says that unless someone gives him something
to do, he doesn't have any thing to say.

One sees five trees, but in the lane there are more than five.

When we made our way past the small farm on the
weekend, it was still there.

Whenever Grandmother would go out, she'd have
the milk can in her hand.

The people in the village, before there were any cars,
used to walk down the middle of the street.

*No one ever sets up a construction site on a Friday.*

The car was in front of the garage. In the evening he'd sit
back in front of the wheel. He'd drive into the garage.

Not on the lakeside, but the land.

A piece of paper with notes slipped out of the book.
It is not the book the paper with the notes belongs to.

In the morning he went to the train station. The following
day, in the afternoon, he came out of the train station.

A good reason to step outside from time to time (Lucky Strike).

Should one finish eating the slightly sour-tasting
hard-boiled egg?

Once he dreamt that he was giving away a lot of money. He did not, however, dream about where all that money had come from, nor what he received in exchange.

One cannot choose the people. If one could, there wouldn't be too many left over.

If you don't say no immediately, it's too late.

Sometimes, when walking by, he pats the goose, which is standing on the stairs, on the head.

He read and didn't understand a thing, but was fascinated all the same.

The old, empty house. Year after year, empty.

We listen to you when you say something too.

One sees someone lean out of their window to see who's in front of the door.

Someone is talking about a neighbour that he knows only from over the fence. Once he saw her on the street. He reluctantly said hello. The neighbour hesitated as well.

It's getting dark. The cars have their lights on. It's early afternoon.

Two invitations have arrived, for the same evening.

There are shirts that one gladly puts on.

Eight in the morning. Who is calling already?

Does one accept here, decline there? Or the other way round?

Do we know each other?

The tram wasn't running. So one walked along the tramlines.

The tank used to be where the taxi stand is today.

He did not want to hear any more, so he simply covered
his ears.

He had studied the instructions.

Military lookout. Sportpalast.

The plane touched the runway. He saw that it did not land.
It increased speed.

The man is training. He knows the reason why.

One knows that they are hunters, the ones shooting
in the woods at night.

Yesterday's people. Tomorrow, you'll be one of them.

Once again an attacker saying, I have to defend myself.

The lamp cannot be repaired. It is old and beautiful.
If we leave it where it is, the room will remain dark.

Someone is on their way to their weekend house. If they've forgotten their keys, they'll have to turn around to get them.

Father always kept a flashlight in his suitcase.

The meteorological reports on the radio. They were reliable. And when they predicted a bombing, soon it was also there.

When the electricity goes, one lights candles.

Come to the window a moment.

He doesn't read any more. He only browses.

Before he entered the hotel room, he received a key ring with six keys. On the way to the room there were three, sometimes four doors to be unlocked.

It is dark, and one feels one's way along the wall until finding the light switch.

In the middle of winter one says, I'm waiting for winter to come.

The closed door one opened, does one really have to close it again?

One can see that there's a difference whether the egg, falling out of one's hand in the kitchen, is raw or cooked.

Something is always falling out of an older person's hands.

Before lying down to sleep, one stops speaking. During the day one doesn't know with what words one will stop speaking.

On his way through town he stopped in front of a window display. Walking on he then turned around and went back.

One sees people who in the meantime have become widowers or widows.

He left early, saying he had things to do. He had nothing to do.

There are people who go and sit in the first row.

The hostess, when in the evening guests are coming, reads all the most important papers in the morning.

Going to the bathroom he noticed a small nail in the wall. He wondered when it was that he had taken down the picture.

He had bought two chairs and taken them away immediately. Now they are out on the street and have to be carried into the house.

When you are old yourself, you treat the old people who are already dead in a friendlier fashion.

Two chairs are standing in front of the table. One feels that two chairs are missing.

Three long-stemmed roses.

At the art market there is art that one can afford.

One can see why the moderator is laughing. Or why they aren't.

A man walks by alone. On the back of his T-shirt, the word Team.

One doesn't hear the painters working. That's why they have the radio on.

If it still ends up raining today, it could also snow.

Come on by again, there's nothing left of the old group.

Are you in good health?

She says that people asking about her is enough.

The wind picks up, and one sees a man running after a plastic bag.

One stone after the other, until all of the stones make a wall.

You just kind of fell into it.

We took a trip to the hills and saw that there was snow. Not a lot of snow, and by the time we turned around to leave, it had begun to melt.

He gave a short account, and his voice sounded impatient.

The new proprietor is the ex-wife of the man who used
to be the proprietor.

She says that she lay the whole night long next to the man. It
was only in the morning that she noticed the man was dead.

She says, If you tell the story, I don't want to be in it.

There are always a few people who try.

*Saturday. Already through another week.*

Simultaneously in the city, on a shore, on the coast.

Into the valleys, yes, not into the depths.

In order to clean up, he'd have to destroy.

After restructuring the house, there were corridors and
rooms which weren't there before. They were waiting to
be used and lived in. Nothing will happen on its own.

He opened the window, there was a draft, and already the
papers began to rustle.

The way to the letterbox is short. One knows that one will
be right back.

One rubs their hands, in the end everything hadn't been
in vain.

When someone disappears and does not reappear,
they remain missing.

One is supposed to explain why a taxi was used.

He looked at the clock and shut his eyes. He opened his
eyes, looked at the clock and realized that, within one
minute, a dozen of unrelated memories had gone through
his head.

If you do not break any thing, you do not have to repair
any thing.

The workman comes with an invoice. We pay it and
continue to sit together for a while.

Not every car is allowed into the city any more.

Every day you have to separate your rubbish, and one
knows that there are four separate bins, one with a grey,
one with a blue, one with a brown, and one with
a yellow lid.

A building burns; officials arrive.

The prisoners were considered traitors.

And if you don't clean up yourself, we will.

He made mistakes, one after the other. But he smiles.
Nothing went wrong.

Are you looking for something here?

Thirty centimetres have disappeared.

One wants to go and drink a beer, but it's late, it's a stormy night, and it's far.

In the past, he was open to everything.

If winter never arrives, one begins gardening sooner.

The man left his wife. She wants to pay him off, so that house remains hers alone. However, with all the money, he wants to buy the house next door and live there with his new girlfriend.

Right away one sees that he's still using the old typewriter.

He plays well. He does not play very well.

The representative's voice was pleasant, she knew it too, and said she would take care of everything.

When he was old, Grandfather had to learn how to use the telephone.

Gnats dancing in the blue air of February.

A sigh of relief. Everything's been paid.

Who is sawing there?

He stands up, looks through the dictionary of foreign words and sits back down.

Precarious neighbourhoods.

The magpie has hopped its way up, branch by branch, and almost reached the crow, which is sitting on the outermost one. It is not moving and does not watch the magpie, which, after a while, swings down and off, fluttering more than flying.

If one dies sooner, one also gives up smoking sooner.

He can still ride a bicycle, he just cannot manage to get on.

You slam your hand, and the gnat is dead. You knew it, you wanted it.

People queuing for a currywurst.

The dimensions are correct; nevertheless, the bed is too small.

He studied all of the documents and knows every detail, and paces back and forth, grumbling.

One drove down a beautiful avenue and really had to pay attention.

Promise. Promise? Promise.

One knows these people from before.

It's cold, one's sitting in the sun.

The apple you see in the painting has the form of an apple
and the colour of an apple.

In the woods one runs into people who are on their way
to their cars, which are parked at the edge of the woods.

A house is being searched, the man living there says
nothing about it.

The man with a lot of money had little money on him.

Having barely won, we don't have to say that we almost lost.

The sun is going down, one is walking through the woods,
and on the path the yellow light from the streetlamps
springing on.

Dark gardens; individual children's voices, fading away
into the houses.

She walked from room to room, on the phone.

One goes shopping. One buys something that was missing.

Investigators drive up, the TV people are already there.

When the technician arrives, one doesn't have to do any thing.

Two new shirts even though one has enough shirts already.

At noon you cannot see the moon.

The sleepers were awoken. They had been asleep for a long time. A few were immediately wide awake and jumped up. Others staggered about and dozed on their feet.

A note was slipped under the door.

Visitors entered the building. Nothing else. They spread out through various rooms.

Having barely lost one said that they had almost won.

*Sundays, when we were at church, there were no bombers.*

Asked who the avant-garde was, he thought of daisies, then crocuses.

He found every book right away. He did not have many books.

In the evenings old people watch old films.

Does one know what was on the note?

He was standing outside the front door and wondering where he was supposed to go.

He ran into an athlete, who had gotten off his racing cycle and was peeling a banana.

The man who fishes bottles out of the bottle bin.

Do you happily recall the person you used to be?

Before he died, he walked up the stairs.

When vertical lines intersect horizontal lines, a chequered field is created.

The problem comes later.

Someone stops by and says hello. One is encouraged to stop by and say hello.

One prepares oneself to be asked questions.

It was raining. All the same, there were a few visitors, most of them completely soaked, only a few had an umbrella, the rain had come unexpectedly, they had actually predicted snow, but it was not cold enough, and the rain had ended soon thereafter.

The problem is there. But it is not our problem.

Why is the car park underwater?

The workers caused some damage. One is waiting for them to come back and repair the damage.

One had experienced it oneself. But what one reads about it is not what one experienced oneself.

Were questions asked?

You come across a platitude. How do you deal with it?

He had gotten upset too soon, and become happy too late.

From time to time it seemed as if someone was living in the empty house.

Why can't it be like it was?

The goodbyes dragged on until one saw one another again.

You'll remain downstairs if you don't come up the stairs.

A comfort, the forsythias.

February's end, the first storm of the year.

The toads wander right across the road. Not all of them reach the other side.

A number of papers saying that the man sitting on stage was smoking a cigarillo.

On the radio a warning, and one doesn't see a lot of people going into the woods.

Once, Father got lost in the mountains. He called for help. The men who came to help him said that they had not heard his voice, but its echo.

If, like he says, you throw a book against the wall three times, in order to continue reading you have to get up three times and pick it back up.

There was one last bit in the jug. Then the jug was empty.

In the afternoon the storm ceases; few trees continue to fall.

We went outside to see if any thing had happened. Around us nothing had happened.

One half is behind you. Now the other half begins.

Once, the fisherman showed up. Later, a second joined him.

He leant against the door and noticed that the door suddenly began to give.

You can stop, but what then?

To hear about a trip, mornings in the snowy mountains, afternoons on the sunny beach.

Asked about which instrument he used to write, to their utter astonishment he said he wrote with a pencil.

He said, I was a bit young, otherwise I would have taken part.

The way through the fields ended in farnland. We carried on until the path began again.

For the way back we sought out another path. In vain. But we knew that there was another path.

There is a new house in the neighbourhood. We have been invited to come see it. We do not intend to go and visit the new house.

He drove into the city, where he walked through the pedestrian mall alone.

The people are friendly. One can prevent them from being so.

One sees a car stopping in front of the door. One does not see anyone get out.

And suddenly he says that he had fallen asleep.

There is no salt in the saltshaker. There is no salt in the entire house.

Someone is talking about current events. It becomes difficult to remain a part of the discussion.

A man goes into the shed and comes back out with the shovel.

One reads what a son has written about his father. What the father forgot, did wrong. Why he roams through the house at night and cannot find his bed.

The light is beginning to change. It is evening, or it is morning.

He kept coughing until he got up and went outside.

The water in the rain barrel is waiting.

Walking into the shop, our butcher asks what brings us
to the butcher's. One says, I'd like to buy a roast. He says,
Then you're in the right place.

One knows how to bring a voice to silence.

Wild geese crying, northwards, in V formation.

The door was open, and we saw the soft, barely visible
drizzle begin to glint in a sudden shaft of sun.

One looks out the window onto the meadow. One looks
up from the meadow towards the window.

Whether the father learnt what his son had written
about him?

A train ride to the north, and one sees the landscape
grow flat.

He slowly grew to be known, he slowly grew to be
unknown.

*Mondays, after a weekend in the country, he began to
arrive later and later, in return he would stay until later
in the evening.*

Smokers will continue dying until they are all extinct.

The hotel was on high ground, and one looked down
onto the bay where the sea began.

He called again in the evening to say that outside it was
bright because of all the string lights, fringing the shore.

One reads of processes in which one is involved but of
which one hears nothing about.

The beanpoles are still there, therefore one does not have to
plant any more. Which Grandfather would have frowned
upon. After picking the beans in autumn, he would pull
them out of the ground, keep them in the shed and plant
them back in the ground in spring. His beanpoles lasted half
his life, ours go rotten after a few years already.

The water coming out of the faucet is so hot that one
has to mix cold water with it.

Digging, one struck tableware. It had probably been buried.

Whenever he made a fire the crows grew silent.

There was no discussion, no decision, the transition came
as if on its own, tea in the morning now and coffee in
the afternoon.

Multiple times throughout the day the zipper opened by itself.

It rings and rings. You just have to remain seated, then
the ringing will stop.

There are people you have not seen in a long time. You try
to count how many. There are always more.

Walking by he saw what was on TV. He did not sit but remained standing for a while, leaning against the doorframe.

He says, If you want, I'll turn on the stove.

The new house is finished, the people have moved in, next to them the next new house is being begun.

Some people have mobile homes. They park in front of the garages where they do not fit.

He cut himself a piece of bread. It was fresh, it had a nice scent. He spread butter across it, and on top of that a piece of salami. He was eating what people call a sausage sandwich.

The stove he wanted to turn on was not off.

A play one saw decades ago. But according to what one reads about the latest production, it was a different piece entirely.

Once the young boy stood in a line for two hours, waiting for bread. By the time he arrived, the bread was gone. The next time he arrived an hour earlier.

After the war we had a goalkeeper, he was also great, with only one arm.

If you run into someone who looks at you with questioning eyes, it could be the roofer, the accountant, the doctor.

The frost was there again, briefly, during the night. In the past it was there, day and night, for weeks.

The tall boy, the one he loved, only came in his winter uniform. He was blond and went to the *Flakhelfer*, and he never saw him again.

Sometimes there were a few leftover sausage ends. The butcher's wife would slip them into his purchase, secretly, for his little dog.

Go on and open your bag.

Before the match we walked over the square and collected the stones.

Bare branches, a flash against a black mass of clouds.

Some people know where the pipes run, but say nothing.

He turns away and says, In the past it wasn't so complicated.

The telephone rings. It can be a warning signal, one needs to know that right away. Most of the time it is not a warning signal.

In the dream sitting in front of a piano, waiting to begin but unable to play piano.

In the following dream unable to find the train station.

He said, With knowledge came fear.

In the shopping cart, more than one can carry with
two hands.

At the edge of town there is the new market. It is big. The
car park is even bigger. But often one drives around the car
park before just stopping and waiting for a space to open.

It is calculated that one has to spend a lot of money to
receive a lot of money.

We were not at home when the chimney sweep came.
Tomorrow we have to be at home. Tomorrow he'll be
coming back.

Someone takes away the chair in which another was sitting.

He always wanted to live somewhere else, now he is
happiest sitting at home.

Looking up he saw swarms of snowflakes dancing,
a spotless sky, the treetops glowing in the light of the setting
sun, a condensation trail split the moon.

There was nothing in the room. He began to look once more.

At night one has aches that one does not have during
the day.

The chimney sweep talks about his daughter. She is a
chimney sweep.

During the night a colleague's name came to mind, someone he had not heard from in quite some time. In the morning he read that he had chosen to end his life.

The cold frame, the windowsill, the wood stack, someone finds everything fantastic.

One doesn't believe him. But he doesn't know. If he did know, what would he do?

We sang and peeled potatoes.

Sometimes he rolled himself a cigarette. Then this and that would occur to him.

In the evenings the smoke in the gardens.

One would meet up and sit on cases of beer.

At the flower shop one doesn't ask for whom the flowers are either.

At times a mood arrives, which makes us silent for a time.

One waits for something to happen.

He pulled out a map. It was an area he knew well. He found the names of a number of places he was unfamiliar with.

Slowly, behind the bushes, a form, moving. It is wearing a bright coat. Just ahead of it a little dog. When the dog pauses, the form pauses too, the one wearing a bright coat.

Ignore the mistake. Maybe it will turn out not to be a mistake.

There are painters who listen to music when they paint.

The jay came and sat on a branch. It looked down at
the birdfeeder. It was empty, and the jay flew away again.

Every hour the headlines. For a while they repeat.
Throughout the day new headlines are added.

The magnolias are white, the hailstones are white.

Going out with a bag filled with sunflower seeds.

Those who did not find a place to sit, sat on the floor.

From the barracks came the sound of Schlager music.

As soon as the door was closed, he would open his
briefcase and take out his spoils.

He brought the bundle of kindling from the construction site.

From the window of the train one could not see the house,
but one could see the two poplar trees behind the house.
They are no longer there.

When the first portable radio appeared, everyone would lie
around the portable radio.

The package was red. The woman was blonde.
The cigarette was Belgian.

The house continued to stand for a while. It had two rooms and was in a garden. It was a garden house.

It began in a bar. It ended in a bar.

*Tuesdays, bright and early, before the rubbish men arrived, he would roll the bins up to the street.*

One complained to the municipality. One is unsure whether the municipality took any notice of the complaint. The municipality is not answering.

You rarely see the green woodpecker. Sometimes you can hear it. It sounds like a green woodpecker who laughs just once, and brief.

No one walks into town any more.

The city is edging ever closer. Many cities are edging closer.

One could not see the fires, but one saw how red the night sky was.

The mayor is not answering.

It is getting cold in the room. One adds some logs. It is getting warm in the room.

What is your favourite flower to be alone with?

He is happy. He has found some meatballs in the refrigerator.

The next surprise. Spreewald pickles.

Speaking he hears that he is speaking.

Two children arrive. The young boy is the young girl's brother. The young girl the young boy's sister.

The white magnolias are brown.

The start has been delayed. The police have reported snowfall. The race organizers do not believe it and send a few people up the mountain roads. They do not get far. The bicycle race will not take place.

You had made up, and then the fight began again.

Busy the whole day but with it the feeling that one is not doing a thing.

There was coffee and cake. He did not like cake.

In truth the trips began even earlier, in that one had to walk to the tram stop.

He sat at the table and fell asleep. When he awoke, he was surprised to find himself sitting at the table.

The friends he no longer had had not been friends.

Now it is snowing again, the whole day. But there is no snow on the ground.

If nothing's going on, one goes back home.

To wear the new shirts for so long that they become old shirts.

Going to an exhibition where, because of all the people, one doesn't see a thing.

The winter fly on the windowpane.

He says, Maybe there won't be any winter next year. She says, Until now, there has always been a winter. He says, It does not have to do with always, but with next winter. She says, Winter is winter.

The telephone company calls to say that they will call two, three times per year.

Children standing on the bridge and throwing snowballs onto the motorway.

The shutter slams. One goes to see whether someone slammed the shutter.

Once, during the night, when the village was ablaze, Auntie called and asked, Is the village on fire?

At home he prefers to have the old sweater on.

In the afternoon he got up and saw, on the distant hills, the sun.

Traces of ancestors that have disappeared. One leads into the neighbouring village, one comes out of the neighbouring village.

Manure is being spread. One cannot tell who is driving the tractor. It is not the old farmer. It is not his one son. It is not the other son.

Wood, says the sign on the road which leads into the woods.

In the morning a neighbour begins to clear away the pile of earth from in front of his house. By the evening he is finished, and the pile of earth is now behind the house.

One knows that when manure is spread, rain is on its way. The manure is not supposed to dry, but to enter the earth with the rain. One sees that it is beginning to rain.

While reading a map it occurs to him that it was when he was a member of the *Deutsches Jungvolk* division of the Hitler Youth that he learnt to read a map.

We didn't say any thing before, when we tried it one more time. As such, no one knew how our first attempt had gone.

One descendent is still alive. A descendent of the old ones who, when the weather changed, heard the lake murmuring. The descendent lives in the hills. He says, When the weather changes, you can hear the lake murmuring.

All of the people came from the one village. Sometimes the lorry was too small. But we had only the one lorry.

The pack of cigarettes was in the kitchen cupboard. The young boy did not know that his uncle counted them. For he never said a thing when, again, a cigarette was missing.

The girl he was not allowed to go out with any longer was said to be a witch.

When the sun would come out at noon, we'd immediately drag out the deckchairs.

Sometimes one begins something as if only continuing.

On the way back, recognizing little.

In the shed we are storing a machine that actually belongs in the rubbish.

In the past one always had ink on one's fingers.

Only one single time do you see the clouds hanging just as they are now.

In the afternoon we would bring the deckchairs back in.

He hesitated to call his son to ask him how things were. He still knew exactly how reluctant he would become whenever his father would call to ask him how things were.

One even thanks the people who did not do any thing.

Once, an Englishman stood at the bar. No problem. Everyone could speak English.

His godmother was a village teacher and had to travel every day from village to village. She drove a heavy Zündapp motorcycle which did not have a light.

Once, Elmar Tophoven told a story about Samuel Beckett finding his way into a revolving door and then, for some time, moving about in a circle until he found his way back out.

Standing in the open window, he raised his hand to wave.

The little *Mainzelmännchen* on his racing cycle moving past.

The woman in the window watches the tree in front of her window being felled.

Some birds, their nests lost.

It does not have to do with the trees. It has to do with the elimination of shade.

Sympathy for Max Raabe who, when asked what his message is, replies that he has no message.

On a bright day the lamp hanging above the table, shining. On the table, beneath the lamp, the cat.

Finally things are moving. One swings oneself back behind the wheel. One has to go fuel up.

First he could not hear too well, then he could not see too well, now he can manage.

One meets up with another. Hasn't been a funeral for a long time, says the one. They're all dead already, says the other.

The kiosk no longer opens at all. No light is on either. In the past a light was always on whenever the kiosk was closed.

But where the picture once hung now hangs another picture.

The woman says, I was three days old when my father planted the tree.

Guests are at the door. They mistook the date. Arrived one week too early.

One is prepared when one knows one has to be prepared.

In winter you see one another more seldom than in summer.

Somewhere in the house a dead bird.

There are a lot of men who still shave in the morning.

Once he said, I've made a lot of mistakes, and all too often I even knew so beforehand.

A buzzard circling. Two buzzards circling.

We have a ladder that does not belong to us. The burglar brought it, used it and then left it behind.

Some people wear sunglasses even when there isn't any sun.

In the dream other people were living in his own apartment.

A house in a picture. If you walk closer, you see two houses.

Many members who attend the general meeting do not
know one another.

The sun is shining, and many cars have their lights on.

One could park here, but you're not allowed to park here.

The deer.

In the glove box tissues, a roll of fruit drops, sunglasses, a
screwdriver, fuel receipts, a piece of wire, a pair of gloves.

The guests ate little. For days now there have been leftovers.

That he did not belong there at all could be seen in his eyes.

At night we could hear the cars.

For a long time one felt safe in the small towns.

As there was no house above the cellar, the people lived
in the cellar.

Rain washed the stones clean.

The morning approaches from the east. The evening
from the west.

We stop at the edge of the village and ask after the filling-station attendant. One doesn't see him any more. Once he said, You don't need a filling-station attendant to get fuel.

Through the pane one could see someone standing
on the mat. He was cleaning off his shoes for a long time.
Then he rang.

Are there any connections? A few.

The off-road vehicle has rusted through. Scrap, says the repair shop, just scrap. But we can still save the kid.

The sky was blue. Then a dark cloud gathered and
it rained and rained until the cloud was gone and the sky
turned blue again.

A blink of the eye was enough.

To talk with himself he goes for a walk.

*It was Monday when he realized that the five previous
days were missing.*

The first sound of spring. A lawnmower.

Tell us everything that happened.

Today the clouds are drifting westwards, and every month
is cruel.

And what do you plan to do afterwards?

One observes rooms that have not been cleaned.

Once, the whole family came to the airport. It was his
first plane trip and everyone wanted to see him one
more time.

At the cinema you see the dead again.

Dreamt that everyone was coming to pick up whatever they
could not get.

When he does not know where to go, he sits down at
his  old table.

The sea in the radio.

By the time we found the exit, it was also the entrance.

To find out when he would have liked to live, he studied
earlier times. He did not find an answer.

During the war, Father's car was up on blocks in the garage.
Sometimes the young boy would sit behind the wheel, his
father had taught him how he would eventually drive. The
young boy would act like he was about to pull out and then
just keep on going, on past fields, lakes and pinewoods, on
down the empty and endless motorway.

Do you know any who still know?

In summer, we hope.

On the left and on the right, road signs announcing deer. On the left-hand sign a deer jumping to the right, on the right-hand sign a deer jumping to the left.

Late at night a plane in which a man is flying home.

The third orchestra was directed by Bruno Maderna.